Little Pleasures

PADDLE CREEK COLLEGE
BOOK THREE

HJ WELCH

Little Pleasures
Paddle Creek College Book Three

Copyright © 2023 by HJ Welch

Cover Design by Cate Ashwood

Also Available

BY HJ WELCH

Paddle Creek College (Daddies and kink)

#1 Heaven Sent

#2 Yes, Sir

Pine Cove (Small town)

Complete Box Set

Homecoming Hearts (Former boy band)

Complete Box Set

Bears-4-U (Daddies and bears multi author shared universe)

Keep Me

BY HELEN JULIET

Contemporary Fairy Tale Adaptations

The Fairy Tale Collection (Beauty and the Beast, Cinderella, Rapunzel)

Daddy's Fairy Tales (Daddies and kink – Goldilocks, Little Red Riding Hood, The Three Little Pigs, Puss in Boots)

Author's Note

This isn't so much a trigger warning as it is an assurance. The dog is absolutely fine. I pinkie promise.

CHAPTER 1
Xander

"YOU'VE CERTAINLY GOT A LOT OF STUFF, HAVEN'T YOU?"

My stepmother's tone might be cheery, but her smile doesn't meet her eyes. I look at the suitcase beside me and the few boxes still in the trunk of my car. Between that and the backpack I'm wearing, I'm not sure I'd consider that 'a lot.'

Then Sunny pulls on her leash, and I realize what Felicia actually means.

"She won't be any trouble, I promise," I say, trying not to let my anxiety get the better of me as I pick up my fluffy best friend and hug her to my chest.

She's only small. No one's really sure what breed she is. Maybe a little Yorkshire Terrier among other things? All I know is she's got big dark eyes, slightly crooked teeth, a tail like a feather duster, and that I love her more that I ever thought it was possible to love anything in this world.

I rescued her this summer before I started the final year of my college degree, and I didn't think she'd be a problem to have in my apartment. But then my greedy landlord decided to change his mind.

Hence why I'm moving back to this house I swore I'd never live in again. However, I'd do anything for Sunny. We might not have known each other long, but I'd sleep on a damned park bench if it meant keeping her, so that's that.

Hopefully, Felicia won't be too unpleasant about the whole thing. It'll just be until I finally finish school and get on my feet. Believe me, I don't want to be living with her any more than she wants to be living with me. This makes the most sense financially, though, and the local college agreed to transfer me just for the last semester.

I need to remember how lucky I am.

"Oof, it's freezing!" my half-brother, Joe, cries as he comes jogging out the front door into the snow. Unlike our step-mother, he's genuinely smiling, and he runs over to me with open arms. "Hey, dude. So glad you're here in time for Christmas. Aww, look at this cutie."

Sunny wriggles in my arms as she wags her tail and tries to lick every inch of Joe's hand. Joe is Dad's son from his first marriage to his high school sweetheart. When that failed, he married my mom and had me. He was already having an affair with Felicia when Mom was going through chemo, and I'm kind of glad she passed before she ever found out.

Unfortunately for me and Joe, she's the one who's hung around. As always, she's smiling at us both like she's trying not to let it show that she just sucked on a lemon.

"Well, let's get in out of the cold, shall we?" she says. "I have people coming over in an hour, and it would be rude to be cluttering up the entrance hall when they arrive."

Great. I haven't even set foot in the house and I'm already getting hints that I'll need to make myself scarce. Well, fine by me. I'll hide in my old room all evening if I can. Maybe Joe might want to play video games or something.

"Hey there!" a cheerful voice calls out from the door, and I turn around to see who's spoken.

Oh. Oh no.

My jaw drops.

Of course in my moment of humiliation, the biggest crush I've ever had in my life comes back to bite me in the ass. Ruben Ward looks as gorgeous as ever as he trots out toward my crappy car and grabs a box. It's so like him to help without even having to be asked and with a smile and everything.

I could almost hate him if I hadn't always loved him.

"H-hey," I manage to stutter to Joe's best friend. They met in high school and were always way nicer than they should have been about letting little me tag along with whatever they were doing, even when they grew up and went to college.

Now I'm the one in college, and this is the first time I've seen Ruben in years.

He's still got those broad shoulders I used to ride on as a kid and then imagined clinging to as a teenager while he did unspeakable things to me. His neat auburn beard looks so soft, and the smile behind it still makes my whole body tingle.

But the way his eyes light up when Joe moves and Ruben can see me properly makes my heart stutter in my chest. "Wow, little dude," he says, shaking his head. "You went and grew up on all of us, didn't you?"

Felicia clicks her tongue, finally letting her irritation show. "Yes, yes, Alexander is a young man now, and everyone's very proud. We're letting all the cold air into the house, so let's move this all inside, hmm?"

Of course, she doesn't lift a finger. She just watches as Joe, Ruben, and I all grab my stuff between us. Then she marches back toward the house, letting the screen door bounce closed behind us.

"Don't worry, I got it," a chipper voice calls as I lock the car and turn to see the others almost at the door.

My younger half-sister, Brigitta, pushes open the screen door for Joe and Ruben, but then her face lights up when she looks out and sees me. Or more specifically, I imagine, sees Sunny.

"Puppy!" she yells, dashing outside. She's all ripped jeans and red pigtails as she launches into the snow. Joe laughs and manages to catch the screen door with his foot before it closes, and he and Ruben carry on inside.

Sunny wags her tail again as Brig approaches, but I still hug her tightly as I don't want her to get too cold.

"Can I pet her?" Brig asks sweetly, and I nod, pleased she hasn't lost her manners in the time I've been gone. Considering she's the offspring of my father and stepmother, Brigitta turned out to be an awesome kid.

"Just be gentle," I say.

Brig rolls her eyes with as much sass as I'm sure any eight-year-old could muster. "No, I was going to yell 'BOO!' at her," she says with a laugh before extremely carefully stroking the top of Sunny's head, where a few snowflakes have collected. "She's so sweet. What's her name?"

"Sunny," I say. That was her name at the shelter anyway, but it was a beautiful summer's day when I adopted her, so I decided to keep it.

"I'll help look after her, I promise," Brig says eagerly, and some of the tension in my chest finally eases. I know it's not going to be as simple as all that moving back here, but I know I'll appreciate any help I can get.

I reach for my suitcase handle, but Brigitta jumps into action. "I've got it!" she cries, despite the thing almost being as big as her. But to her credit, she diligently drags it over the driveway to the steps of the house, where Joe kindly hurries down and swiftly takes it off her hands. That just leaves me to bring Sunny inside.

I exhale as we close the front door and finally get out of the snow. Mind you, the temperature of the house might be better than outside, but I wouldn't say the entrance hall was exactly *warm*. The whole house has the same cold, showroom feel to it, with marble floors and chrome finishings. Even the Christmas decorations are all black and silver with bluish-white LED lights. I shiver as I place Sunny down, praying that she doesn't get overexcited and try and pee on anything.

It's almost like time travel. In a second, I'm eighteen years old again and still afraid to touch anything even though this is supposed to be my damn house. When I place Sunny down, her nails skitter on the hard floor and seem really loud.

"So, Big G?" Joe says as he sets the suitcase down near the foot of the stairs.

Brigitta looks up from where she's petting Sunny again, and grins at him. "Yeah?"

Joe raises a skeptical eyebrow. "Dad said you were the third alternate at the Little Miss Paddle Creek Christmas Pageant. Is that true?"

I can see why he was sounding skeptical. That doesn't sound like her at all. I turn to see her scowling as Joe throws me a conspiratorial grin. "Mom told me it was a spelling bee. That's the only reason I agreed to wear that stupid dress." Then her face brightens. "I came fourth, though, cuz my talent was reciting the whole periodic table from memory."

Joe and I laugh. "Atta girl," Joe says, hugging her to him as they both wander down the hallway toward the kitchen.

I stand on the front doormat, feeling awkward and probably making a puddle. Sunny looks up at me quizzically, and I let out a heavy sigh. "I don't know what to do, either," I admit. "But this is home for now."

"Hey," a soft, deep voice says from above, and my heart leaps into my throat as I see Ruben coming down the stairs from where he must have helped Joe with my stuff. My face burns, thinking about him seeing my teenage bedroom and all the embarrassing Below Zero posters I have up, not to mention my toy dinosaur collection. "It's nice to see you again, Xander."

Of course he remembers that I always preferred to be called that instead of my full name. Honestly—why does he have to be so *perfect*?

I bite my lip as he comes face to face with me and somehow manages to slip his hands into the jeans that are hugging his thick thighs tightly. He smells faintly of motor oil, I guess because he owns a repair shop, but there's also that woodsy smell I'd forgotten until this very second that makes my mouth water.

Fuck! No! Stop! He's over ten years older than me. He probably still thinks of me as a dumb kid. I need to get a grip before I embarrass myself.

"It's nice to see you, too," I say with as much of a smile as I can manage when I'm feeling so anxious and nervous. God, I'm wound up so tightly with stress I feel like I might explode. I need to escape before I put my foot in it. "I, uh, better get my case out of the way before I upset Felicia any further."

He snorts and glances toward the kitchen, where voices are drifting our way, then back at my case. "Do you want a hand?" he asks, because he's a gentleman, so of course he does.

I shake my head. "That's okay," I tell him, feeling flustered. "You've already helped me."

He grins. "There's no expiration date on help," he says with a wink before grabbing my bag anyway. I open my mouth to protest, but he's already turned to go back up the stairs, so there isn't much left for me and Sunny to do except follow him.

I try not to watch Ruben's ass as I trail up the stairs after him or notice how his muscles flex as he carries my heavy case with just one hand. I can see them bulging under his lumberjack shirt, and my knees feel weak as I imagine what it might be like to have them wrapped around me.

I'm jolted out of my extremely inappropriate thoughts as he goes into the room that I know is mine, but the second I look through the open door, I realize I don't recognize a single thing.

Wow. Okay. At least I don't have to be embarrassed about the boy band posters that used to be there. They're all gone, as is every other personal item of mine. The walls have been repainted, and there's new carpet to go with the bedsheets that look like they've never been slept in, all in masculine tones of blue.

I've been completely erased.

"I'll leave you to get settled," Ruben says kindly, and I wonder if he senses what I'm feeling. Does he have any idea how wrong-footed I am right now? Where's all my stuff? Did my entire childhood just get thrown into the trash?

"Thank you," I manage to utter, jutting my chin toward the suitcase.

"Anytime," he says. He lingers in my doorway for a few more seconds, then gives me a smile and heads back downstairs.

I slump onto the bed, and Sunny immediately jumps up beside me, and puts her head in my lap. I take her leash off and stroke her head, thinking that she's most likely not allowed on the navy bedspread, but that thought is about the only thing to cheer me up in this moment.

I'm not wanted here. I don't belong here. But this is the way it has to be for a little while if I'm going to keep Sunny and stop myself from drowning in debt. I'm lucky I have a family who will take me in, even if I know it will come with strings attached.

Right now, I'm just grateful to have my best girl by my side, and I try not to linger too long on the complicated tangle of thoughts floating in my head that centers around one Ruben Ward. I'm sure he's just here for the evening. Joe hasn't lived here for years, after all. They're both only here for Felicia's party, I'm sure. And I don't think I actually embarrassed myself when I was speaking with him just now, so it's probably all fine.

I simply need to get through tonight, and Ruben can stay my secret crush forever more. He'll never be any the wiser.

CHAPTER 2

Ruben

WHOA.

I was not expecting that.

I'm glad to have a minute to myself as I slowly make my way back downstairs toward the kitchen, where Joe and his family are congregating. Well, his dad's side of the family, anyway. His mom moved a couple of hours away when Joe went off to college and got his own car. I think sticking close to Paddle Creek to share custody of him just about killed that poor woman. Seeing your ex remarry twice must be awful.

Which brings me back to Xander. The last time I saw him, he was all big ears and knobbly knees, always with his nose stuck in a comic book and nails dirty from rescuing worms in the back yard.

Now he's a man. And he's beautiful.

He's still wound up tighter than a spring, though. I remember he was always an anxious kid, and it pains me to see he's just as stressed despite growing up.

It frightens me how much I want to wrap him up in my arms and make all his troubles disappear.

That's my best friend's kid brother I'm talking about, though, not some boy I've met at a club or on an app. No matter how strongly my Daddy instincts are rearing their heads, I have to quash them down. There are some lines that can't even be considered crossing.

I pause before reaching the kitchen, taking a breath and giving myself a shake. It's fine. I was just taken by surprise. Sure, I knew Xander was coming home, but my heart hasn't stopped thumping since I laid eyes on him. However, there's no harm done. The shock will fade, and I probably won't see him again for another few years.

Joe hardly ever comes back to this house, preferring to spend the holidays with his mom, but he's always felt protective of Xander and wanted to make sure he settled in okay with Felicia and their dad being like they are. If Joe's not going to be here, then I won't have any excuse either.

I ignore the fact that it makes me kind of sad.

"Hey, man. Want a beer?" Joe asks as I amble into the kitchen, which looks more like a deck of a starship than it does a place to lovingly prepare a family dinner. Indeed, Felicia has gotten caterers in as usual to provide for her party guests. She's currently unwrapping platters of finger food that looks delicious, but I know better than to pick at.

"Uh, I'll take a Coke if you've got one?" I say, as I'm driving.

Joe seems to be on my wavelength. He passes me a can, then sidles up to me so he can lean in and murmur, "Once I'm happy Xander's okay, feel like blowing this Popsicle stand and heading over to O'Toole's?"

I grin and tap my can against his bottle. I'll happily drive us to Paddle Creek's best—only—queer pub. We can walk back to my place from there, and I feel like we both need to blow off a little steam.

When I came out as gay to Joe in college, I was kind of

terrified it would be the end of our friendship. Not only was he totally cool with it, but he also actually got the guts to come out to me as bisexual a couple of years later. I really did hit the best buddy jackpot.

So I seriously need to stop my brain from wandering back to his little brother.

"O'Toole's sounds great," I say honestly. "Did you want to check on Xander first? I helped him take his case to his room…"

I let the implication of that statement linger. Joe's face was slack with shock when he realized what Felicia had done. He'd never really had a room in this house, just one for a couple of years before college, so it wasn't that much of a surprise they turned it into a guest bedroom.

But having that one spare meant there was no reason to gut Xander's room like they did other than out of total spite. When Joe asked Felecia what happened, she said she'd donated it all to charity in a tone that suggested she definitely considered herself a saint for doing so instead of a heartless monster. I can only hope that Xander took all the things he really cared about with him.

Joe presses his lips together, then shakes his head. "I don't want to overwhelm or baby him," he says in response to my question about Xander. "He's probably got a lot to process. If he comes down, we can chat. If not, I'll message him and tell him to let me know if there's anything he needs or something he wants to talk about or whatever."

I nod, letting that attitude guide me, as my instincts are screaming at me to do the opposite. I want to cuddle him, to tell him this is just a blip and things will get better, to yell at his stepmom for being so heartless and clearly unwelcoming. But Joe is thinking clearly, and my caveman brain needs a chance to calm down.

We hang out on the edge of the kitchen for a little longer.

Brigitta peacefully reads a book while Felicia runs around like she's a commander preparing for a life-or-death battle rather than hosting a couple dozen people for holiday drinks. Her stress is grating on my nerves, as is the click-clacking of her heels on the tiled floor. Xander doesn't show his face—unsurprisingly—and I figure it'll be better to head out now before the guests start arriving and block my truck in the driveway.

Joe and I are preparing to take our leave just as Felicia starts losing her shit because Brigitta is refusing to put a dress on. Felicia threatens to send Brigitta to her room so she'll miss the whole party, and Brigitta runs out of the kitchen so fast her mom is practically left standing in her dust. I don't need Joe to signal me that this would be an excellent exit cue for us as well, lest Felicia turns her wrath our way. Honestly, when I have buddies over, I can't wait for them to arrive. You'd think Felicia was being made to do community service.

I'd find it strange that Joe and Xander's dad isn't around, but that guy is nothing but a work-shy charmer who will no doubt show his face at the last minute and take all the credit. I try not to be prejudiced against anyone, but Mr. Patterson is the most stereotypical used car salesman I've ever met in my life.

Joe exhales and shakes his head as he sits in the passenger seat of my Ford F-150. "Sorry about that, man."

I shrug, then turn the ignition key. "Hey, you were there for Xander. That's all that matters."

Joe drums his fingers on his knee. "I just wish I could do more."

"He's only going to be there for a short while," I assure him as I start driving us into town. The little Hawaiian lady hanging from the rearview mirror jiggles her hips as the truck moves. Normally, I'd park at my place and walk to the pub, but in this weather, I figure it'll be better to get our asses indoors now, then head back to my place with beer jackets on to help us keep warm.

O'Toole's is set a little off the beaten track by the creek this town gets its name from. The lot is pretty full, which is normal, considering it's a weekend close to Christmas. Sometimes I much prefer it when it's dead and I can have a quiet beer without having to deal with anyone else. But tonight, I feel like losing myself in a cacophony of voices and some classic rock music.

I take a deep breath in as we cross the parking lot, inhaling the cold air and the scent of pine from the surrounding trees. Paddle Creek isn't exactly a bustling city, but I do appreciate that in corners like this, it's so quiet and close to nature.

"First round's on me," Joe announces as we step through the door into the warmth, the wall of sound hitting us like a wave on a beach. I grin and look around at the mostly male crowd. There's something about queer spaces that just makes me feel relaxed in a way nowhere else can. I can't say I've particularly had much trauma in my life, thank goodness. But I still feel incredibly safe in places like this.

"Gentlemen," Donna the bartender says as we approach. She's a gruff leather dyke who doesn't take anyone's shit. She has, however, slipped me more free beers than I can count because I keep her Harley Davidson purring like a kitten. "What can I get you?"

The question is more or less redundant, but Joe holds up two fingers and winks at her. She scoffs, but secretly I think she loves a bit of flirting. She cracks open two beer bottles for us, sets them on the bar, then takes Joe's card to start a tab. I'll pay him back tomorrow—it's just easier that way. We've known each other for so long we don't have to check things like that.

"Cheers," I say as we clink the glass together.

Then I jut my chin across the room. Most of the guys here are sitting around shooting shit. There are a few people at the pool table, and some are playing darts or watching the game on the TV. But Donna has moved to talk to a guy called Nim at the end of the bar. From my work, I know he's also a motorcyclist, so perhaps they're friends through that. He's new-ish around town, and he radiates a 'fuck off' sort of vibe that means I've only ever spoken to him about his bike or occasionally ordered a coffee from his cat café in town.

Right now, though, he appears to be nursing a pint of Guinness as he bottle feeds a tiny ball of fluff that he's got bundled up on the bar top. The bottle of milk is barely bigger than his thumb, and he's concentrating with all his might on the tufty little thing. When Donna asks him a question, he doesn't look up. He just grunts in response, and she laughs, moving on to serve other patrons.

I grin at the unusual sight, but when I turn back to look at Joe, he's chewing his lip and frowning at his bottle as he scratches at the corner of the label.

"Everything okay?" I ask.

He gives me a one-armed shrug and sighs before finally looking back up at me. "Sorry. I'm just worrying about Xander. I know he's not a little kid anymore, but living with that woman is enough to shake anyone's mental health, even as an adult. She always picked on him for being gay."

I offer him a small smile and squeeze his shoulder. One of the reasons he was determined to come out as bi in college, even though he'd never dated or had sex with a man back then, was because he wanted to stand in solidarity with Xander. Felicia was always much less likely to start a fight with Joe than she was with Xander, and when he made his sexuality common knowledge, it was as if he took a big chunk of her ammunition away.

But I know what he means. That woman will take any chance she gets to chip at that poor boy's already damaged self-esteem, and the thought tears me up inside.

Which is probably why my mouth opens before my brain can intervene. I can't even blame the beer. I haven't had a sip yet.

"Hey, I can keep an eye on him while he's here," I volunteer. "You know, check in and stuff."

As soon as the words leave my mouth, I know it's a terrible idea. The last thing I need to be doing is spending more time with that sweet, gorgeous young man, especially without Joe there acting as a buffer. But the way Joe's face lights up in delight tells me I absolutely can't walk the offer back.

"Really? Would you?" he asks. "Dude, that would set my mind at ease, for real. I can give you his number, if you like?"

I only hesitate for a fraction of a second before I smile and nod, getting out my phone. It's fine. I can be a grown up about this. It's a favor to my best and oldest friend. I won't abuse the number to get too close to Xander or anything creepy like that. I'll be like another brother to him.

Definitely not his Daddy.

CHAPTER 3
Xander

"Welcome to Dino-Mite! How many in your party today?"

I manage to keep the smile on my face and the pep in my voice as I greet the next group of guests to enter the restaurant. I might be dead on my feet, but I'm determined to make this experience as pleasant as possible for the adults in the group who look twice as tired as I feel. Looking at the dozen or so screaming five-year-olds surrounding them, I can't say I blame them.

"Uh, we have a booking for Noah's birthday," one of the women says.

I assumed that was the case from looking at the calendar, but I've been so nervous filling in for the host today that I've been triple checking everything. When Hilary called in sick with food poisoning, my manager begged me to cover for her, even though I usually only bus tables. I'm too shy to be a natural people person, but I could see how stressed she was, so I agreed to help her out. Plus, she said I'd get extra pay, which definitely helps.

I grab a couple of the adults' menus, a stack of paper kids' ones, and a couple of boxes of crayons to go with them and beam at the woman. "Right this way. You're in the Cretaceous Corner."

"YES!" a little boy near the front says as he punches the air. Judging by the number of 'I am five!' badges he's wearing, I'd guess this is Noah. "That's when the tyrna...tyrnao...when the T-rex was alive!"

I grin at him, not feeling like I have to put on any sort of front. "That's right," I say as I start leading them through the restaurant. I tap the baseball cap that's part of my uniform. It has triangular teeth on the rim and googly eyes on the front of the hat. "Do you know what kind of dinosaur the tyrannosaurus was?"

"A meat-eater!" Noah bellows, setting off all the other kids roaring and trying to bite each other. Their noise is lost amid the hordes of other children in the restaurant, the dings and whirls coming from the arcade games, and the atmospheric jungle soundtrack playing through the speakers.

Yes, I might have to take painkillers after most shifts to deal with the headaches. The carpet is threadbare and sticky, and the eighties era play area barely passed its last health and safety inspection. But I love the fake fossils molded into the walls. The neon green plastic seats and tables ruin any kind of illusion of authenticity they might have been striking for forty years ago, but they're so easy to wipe clean.

But the best—the very *best*—part is that kids just run riot here. Yes, it's chaotic, and there are daily tears, tantrums, and Technicolor yawns, but there is also freedom.

The kind of freedom I only remember from before my mom got sick.

The kids don't even bother sitting down when we reach the long party table. They just run for the soft play zone and the ball pit. I hand the woman who seems to be in charge the collection of menus. "Would you like party platters for the table?" I ask her. "We work it out to share, and it's thirteen dollars per kid. We've got cheese and tomato pizzas, dino chicken nuggets, a ton of fries, mini cheeseburgers, bottomless soft drinks, and a bowl each for the ice cream bar." I tap the top menu. "And *this* is the grown-ups' menu."

The food options are mostly just bigger portions of the kids' stuff, but where I pointed to has a list of ridiculously named and surprisingly strong cocktails.

The woman's face lights up. "We'll start with three Mesozoic Margaritas," she says, and the other man and woman with her nod eagerly.

I grin, feeling good that I've helped their crazy day in a small way. "Coming right up."

I know I'm supposed to just seat them, but the server covering that area is rushed off his feet. So I grab him when he's got a second and relay the order, and I'm happy when he looks relieved. That's the other nice thing about working here. It might be old and tacky, but the team looks out for each other, and we all split the tips fairly.

There's nobody waiting at the front door for the moment, so I take a breather and lean against the small desk, rubbing my tension-filled forehead. I've got three hours left on shift until I can get home to my baby girl. She'll need a quick walk, and then I can try my best to get that paper done that's due tomorrow.

I never should have started this degree. It should have taken me four years, but I've had to stop a couple of times so I could work enough to save up and afford it. I'm going to be twenty-five this year, and I'm still waiting to start my life because I refuse to quit.

I know it's more money to finish it, but I feel so strongly that if I give up now, that will be so much more of a waste. Besides, I absolutely love everything I'm studying to get this Bachelor of Arts. English, classics, philosophy, even a little drama, which I low-key hated, but I am proud I made it through that class. If I can just hang in there a little longer, I'll not only have the degree, but also something that's truly *mine*.

Something my father and stepmom can never take away from me.

At least in Albertson, I only had to juggle work and school. I shared my apartment with a couple of other guys, but we all mostly kept to ourselves.

Now when I go home, I have to contend with Felicia as well.

I sigh heavily, my headache getting worse, so I sneak a few mouthfuls of water from my bottle behind the counter, hoping hydration will help. I don't understand why my stepmom doesn't just leave me alone. It's not like I try and get in her hair—the complete opposite, actually. I even keep Sunny in my room except for when I'm taking her out to walk.

But it's like because I'm back under her roof, she thinks she has a right to know everything I'm doing and—worse—try and control it.

I keep telling myself that it could be much bleaker. All that matters is that I get to keep Sunny. I'll suffer anything for that. And it's only supposed to be temporary, but Felicia and my dad decided *after* I moved in that I needed to pay them rent. They are honestly loaded, and I was shocked they'd make me do that when they know I'm already on my knees with student debt. But I guess that's how my dad got rich in the first place. By being a penny-pinching bastard.

I'd have thought they'd want me to save up and move out as soon as I graduate. But at this rate, I'll be living with them until I'm thirty.

I shudder at the prospect.

I'm so lost in my troubled thoughts that I don't spot the

single diner coming through the door until they're practically on top of me. I snap my attention back, the words already tumbling out of my mouth. "Welcome to Dino-Mite! How can I…" My voice dies.

It's Ruben Ward.

I know my jaw drops, but I can't seem to pick it back up again. I haven't seen him since that day I moved in several weeks ago before Christmas. However, Joe obviously gave him my number and told him to keep an eye on me or something. He's been texting me for weeks, and I've been too mortified to respond. He still thinks I'm some little kid with skinned knees who can't take care of himself, and here I am lusting after him like a dog in heat. It's too much. I thought he would politely get the hint that I don't want him fussing over me, but apparently, he's just as stubborn as he always was.

"H-hi," I manage to stammer, probably going bright red underneath my silly dinosaur hat. Shit. It's like he's purposefully looking for embarrassing situations to find me in. Even so, I can't deny what a thrill it is to see him again. Fuck, he's just so ridiculously handsome. I want to climb him like a tree.

I bite my tongue and try not to cringe at myself. Yeah, right. Like I'd have the confidence to do that. I've had a fair few sexual encounters in my life, but they've ranged from pretty okay to downright awful, and most of the time, I'm just terrified of being good enough and getting the guy to come. There has been more than one occasion where they haven't even cared if I got off or not.

So no, I need to keep my Ruben-centered sexual fantasies under lock and key unless I want to humiliate myself any further. I bet a powerhouse of a man like that has guys falling over themselves for him.

"Hey, Xander," he says in that low rumble that makes

my knees weak and has done since I hit puberty. Fuck. I would have hoped this silly crush would have lessened in the time we've been apart, not come back with a vengeance.

"Hi," I say again, managing not to stutter this time. I want to ask him what he's doing here. I assume he's not getting lunch. But that would be rude. "Can I, um, help you?" Mercifully, no other patrons have arrived since he did, but I still don't want to get caught talking to someone when I should be working.

He grins and shrugs as he slips his hands into his jeans which—like before—just drags my attention to his thick thighs. I bet they're strong and hairy. I wonder what they'd feel like—

NO! Stop it, Alexander.

"I was worried about you," Ruben says bashfully. "You didn't respond to my texts. I didn't want to bother you, but I promised Joe I'd stay in touch. What with Felicia being like she is and all."

I try to stop my heart from sinking. Of course that's the reason he's here. I knew it. However, deep down, I was hoping there was the tiniest chance that he was here because he wanted to see *me*. But that's ridiculous.

"Oh, I'm fine," I say with a wave of my hand, but to my absolute and complete horror, my voice cracks on the word 'fine.' I cough, and tears spring to my eyes.

You know, just in case I wasn't embarrassed enough and needed another reason for the ground to swallow me up before I could possibly lower this man's opinion of me any further.

"S-sorry," I splutter, and try and shake it off with a laugh as I hastily wipe my face. "I'm just tired."

I expect him to get awkward or annoyed, but instead, he just looks incredibly concerned. "I know. Joe said you were studying and working all hours. Are you getting any time off at all?"

I bite my lip and look away. "Yeah," I say, but even to my own ears, it sounds uncertain. "I walk Sunny every day."

Ruben huffs and shakes his head at me. "And that's wonderful—you're obviously a caring owner, and walking is good for you're and physical health. But that's also a responsibility. Are you taking time to just chill? You know—watch movies and play video games or whatever?"

I open and close my mouth, a lump rising in my throat as the hot tears threaten to come back. Does he really care that much about me? What does it matter to him if I'm burning the candle at both ends?

"It's, uh, it's just until I finish college," I say.

He raises an eyebrow, and not only do my knees weaken again but my cock definitely throbs between my legs. Why does that stern look suddenly make me want to melt into a horny puddle?

"Yes, but you have to survive college and pass your exams first," he says in a no-nonsense tone that does nothing to help with my boner situation. "Self-care is important."

"O-okay," I say. I'm not sure why. It's not like I can magic up extra hours in the day.

"Are you at least eating properly?" he asks. "Brigitta told Joe that Felicia doesn't like cooking for you if you're not around for regular mealtimes."

My cheeks definitely burn in shame at that. Brig is a snitch, but she's not wrong. Felicia doesn't like me using her kitchen, either, so there has been a lot of quick, microwave ramen in my life lately, which I know has the nutritional value of cardboard. Luckily, I get fed here at reduced rates, but again, it's more grease than anything else.

"I'm fine," I mumble again, unable to look him in the eye in case I let those tears finally break free. Thankfully, some actual customers come in, and Ruben steps aside to let me greet them. I force a smile, but I know it doesn't meet my eyes, so I'm glad to find them a table quickly and leave them to their waitress.

When I come back, Ruben is not only still there for some unholy reason, but he's frowning, and my insides turn to jelly in a bad way. *No, no, no!* I don't want him to be mad or disappointed with me!

"Look," he says firmly as I return to the host's plinth. His arms are crossed over his broad chest, and he looks so solid, like a brick wall. "Joe's my best buddy, and I promised him I'd watch out for you. I know you didn't respond to my texts, and the last thing I want to do is smother you. You're an independent young man now, I get it. But I'm worried about you. I'd really like it if you came over to my place sometime soon so I can cook you a proper dinner. I don't mind helping out walking Sunny, either. Being my own boss means my work hours are pretty flexible."

My jaw is hanging open once more. I shake my head faintly, warring with my emotions. "I don't want to be a bother," I whisper, but inside me, fireworks are going off. Did Ruben just really offer to make me dinner and walk my dog? Not once, but regularly? That's...that's one of the nicest things anyone's ever said to me.

He shrugs, but he's smiling. "Joe and I have been buddies forever. I think now you're an adult too, there's no reason we can't be actual friends as well, right? We always got along when we were younger. I'd like to be your friend, Xander. But if I'm overstepping, I can—"

"No!" I cry, then glance around in embarrassment. Luckily, it doesn't look like anyone else noticed over the din in the restaurant. "I mean...no, you're not overstepping. I...well, I'd like to be friends, for sure. I don't really know anyone here in town anymore."

Ruben beams, and my heart aches. He claps me on the shoulder. "Awesome. Or should I say 'roar-some'?" he asks with a grin, looking around at the tacky but cute décor.

"Roar-some," I repeat, loving how warm that silly pun makes me. "I'll, um, text you my schedule," I offer, still not believing this is really happening.

But Ruben nods, looking pleased with himself. "I'll be waiting to hear from you, Xander. Take care."

I wave faintly as he heads back outside into the parking lot.

Did I just become friends with my teenage crush?

I think I did.

I'm not sure yet if that's a good or a bad thing, but it's apparently happening whether I want it to or not. So I might as well lean into it, right?

CHAPTER 4
Ruben

It's a good thing that I'm the boss because on days where my head is full of nothing but cotton candy—like, say, today—I can leave whenever the hell I want.

Don't get me wrong. Usually, I'm the first in and last out. I love working here at the garage, and when old man Horowitz insisted that I took it over when he retired, I thought I'd hit the jackpot. I seriously get paid to tinker around with all kinds of engines day in and day out. I reckon I must have been a saint in a past life to get that lucky.

But today, the banging and clanging is setting my teeth on edge. The radio seems too loud, and my hands are twitchy. I tried changing from manual labor to accounting on the computer, but that was even worse. The numbers were just floating in front of my eyes. I think it's time that I accept defeat and sneak off to make sure my head is in the right space for this evening.

Except there is never any sneaking off in Horowitz's.

A sharp whistle pierces through the air before I even make it across the workshop to the front door. I sigh and turn around to see Leandra push out the creeper she's lying on from underneath a Ford Focus.

"Yo, boss," she cries with a grin as she sits up. "Where you sneaking off to?"

I huff. "I'm not sneaking," I say, trying not to sound grumpy. "I'm just leaving."

Leandra just grins harder, though. "If you were 'just leaving,' you would have given us shit before heading out." She waggles a grease-stained wrench at me. "You, my friend, are sneaking."

"Come on, spill," Trey says as he pokes his head out from under the hood of an electric blue Honda Civic. "You've got a date, haven't you?"

I growl under my breath. The trouble with my team is that most of them are married or in serious relationships. Hell, Trey and his husband *also* have a boyfriend, the greedy fucks. So that means my love life is often subject to heavy speculation. Usually, I don't mind, but today it touches a nerve.

"Definitely not a date," I growl, crossing my arms over my chest.

Leandra snorts. "It's so a date."

"Go on, boss," Lewis urges me as he comes out of the office. He's got the company iPad in his hands, but he's giving me all his attention, just like the rest of this nosy lot. "Give us a hint. It's been ages since you went on a date."

I wince at his bluntness. Yeah, I do know that. It's been a good while since I've had anything more than a hookup or gone down to Indianapolis to do a scene. I guess that's exactly *why* it's been so long. I seem to have no trouble finding boys for a night, but what I want is a full-time commitment. The real deal, twenty-four seven.

But after a string of boys who weren't interested in being Daddied outside of the bedroom, I lost heart. It's been over five years since my previous boyfriend lived with me. When things broke down and he moved out, I closed up his play-room and tried not to think about what was behind that door since.

"It's not a date," I repeat, trying to sound firm, but I'm worried it comes out sounding a little sad. "I'm just doing my best friend a favor."

I say it out loud to remind myself of that as much as to inform them. I know inviting Xander over for dinner was a dangerous idea, but I just couldn't stop myself. The thought that he's not eating properly—even worse that his step-mother is trying to starve him—filled me with a rage I couldn't control. It was either invite him over so I could take care of him or punch a triceratops on the nose.

Besides, this is exactly what Joe asked me to do. I'm looking after his brother by giving him a decent meal. I fully intend to help with walking his sweet dog, too. There's nothing untoward going on here. *It's not a date.*

"Aww, boss, we're just messing with you," Trey says with a nod. "Have a good evening."

"Yeah, a *good* evening," Leandra adds with a wink.

I sigh and shake my head good-naturedly. They mean well and genuinely want me to be happy, but the situation is complicated.

Because I just can't stop thinking about Xander.

If he wasn't Joe's half-brother, I probably would be considering what a relationship might look like between us. He's screaming to be cuddled and taken care of in a way I know I could do perfectly. And he's so fucking *gorgeous*. Big hazel eyes and dark hair that I want to run my fingers through and lips I could kiss for hours. I know there's an age gap—bigger than with anyone else I've dated before—but that doesn't bother me if it wouldn't bother him. One of the best things about being a Daddy is imparting wisdom and having the life experience to take charge of situations.

But that way of thinking is redundant. Worse than that, it's dangerous. I simply cannot cross that line. Xander is vulnerable, and I'd never be able to look Joe in the eye again if I took advantage of his little brother.

So that's that. I'm just going to give him a taste of home away from home. The point of inviting him over is to offer some respite from work, school, and that terrible woman who haunts his house like a banshee.

It's a short drive across town to my place. Seeing as I've now got an extra hour before Xander arrives, I decide to make my mother's mustard stuffed chicken instead of the simpler meal I had planned. It takes about half an hour to get the cheesy mustard mix stuffed into the chicken breasts and wrap them with bacon. I can let it bake until Xander arrives, filling my small house with the tasty, inviting aroma, then I'll just need to add the veg.

I'd already spent some time tidying over the past few days since I saw him at Dino Mite. But suddenly, it doesn't seem good enough, so I get the vacuum cleaner out and attack all the carpets and even the bathroom. I've wiped down the entire kitchen, but now I'm peeling potatoes and trying not to make too much more mess. When the doorbell rings, I take a deep breath and dry my hands on a dishcloth.

"It's *not* a date," I mutter to myself as I stride toward the front door.

All sensible thought leaves my head, though, once I open the door. Xander is anxiously hugging himself on the porch, practically trembling and biting his lip. He's gripping Sunny's leash despite the fact that she's sitting patiently by his feet. Her tail is wagging like crazy, and when she sees me, she jumps to her feet but she doesn't tug. I'm not sure what kind of dog she is. Probably a mix of several breeds that resulted in the fluffy little caramel brown thing that she is.

"Hi," I say brightly, genuinely so happy to see him. After the way he avoided my texts, I thought he might bail at the last minute. I'm so glad he's here. He doesn't have to worry about anything now, that's my job. The sooner I ease that frown from his face, the better.

"Hey," he says, his voice quivering with just that one word. This poor boy is run ragged and is one misstep away from breaking down in tears, I'm sure.

"Come on in," I say warmly, extending my arm toward the hallway.

My house isn't any kind of palace, but it's all mine, and I'm very grateful for it. It's an honor to share it with anyone, but especially him tonight. People should always feel safe in their homes, and I know he doesn't have that right now, but he can have it with me, even just for a little while.

"Thank you for this," he stutters before he even manages to get his shoes off. "It's really kind of you. I can pay you back for—"

"Whoa, whoa, whoa," I say, throwing my hands up and shaking my head. "Whenever you're here, you're my guest, okay? You're welcome any time, and it's my pleasure to be your host. I don't get to cook much for other folks these days, so this is a treat for me, all right?"

He swallows and looks around before meeting my gaze once more. "Yeah?"

"Yes," I assure him. "Do you want to come through to the kitchen? We can let Sunny out into the yard to run around if you like. I already checked all the fences to make sure there wasn't anywhere she could squeeze through and escape."

He blinks at me. "That's so thoughtful of you," he says incredulously. I shrug, but I guess he's not used to people in his life being thoughtful.

"This way," I say with a smile, leading him down the hall into my kitchen. As promised, I let them both out into the back yard, where Sunny immediately starts zooming around like a maniac.

A small laugh escapes Xander's mouth, startling him. "She doesn't get much free time these days," he admits.

A warmth spreads through my chest. "She's welcome here any time," I assure him. "You both are."

He bites his lip again and looks at me through those long, dark lashes. "I know you're Joe's best friend, but you don't have to go out of your way for me, I promise. He wouldn't expect that."

I snort. "I'd take a bullet for that asshole," I say with a grin. "Hanging out with you is going to be fun, I know it. You're not a burden, Xander."

His expression suggests he thinks otherwise, but he doesn't say anything, at least.

We leave the back door open so Sunny can come and go as she pleases, and I get Xander settled at the kitchen table while I finish off making the buttery mashed potatoes to go with the chicken and steamed green veggies. Proper comfort food for the soul, that is.

"Can I get you a glass of wine or a beer?" I offer, thinking it might help him relax and unwind.

"Oh, that's so nice of you, but I'm driving."

Before I can stop myself, my mouth is moving again without my brain's permission. The trouble is what's best for him is outweighing what's sensible, considering the strong attraction I'm feeling.

"You're more than welcome to stay here for the night," I volunteer. "The sofa folds out into a pretty decent bed. The whole point is to get a real break from your stepmom, right?"

His mouth drops open but then a delicate pink blush

creeps onto his face. He bites his lip, but that can't contain his smile. *Yes!* Score one for Ruben.

"That sounds like a tropical vacation right about now," Xander says with a chuckle. "Felicia is getting even more...*Felicia* at the moment since her sister's wedding is coming up. A break could do us all good."

I remember Joe mentioning something about having to go to a wedding because he was certain that anyone related to his stepmom was definitely going to be a bridezilla. I wince, feeling for Joe, Xander, and Brigitta having to get caught up in all that. But it makes me even more determined to give Xander somewhere to escape to.

"So, that's a yes?" I prompt gently.

Xander considers a second. "Um, okay then. Yes. If you're sure it's not an imposition."

I shake my head. "I think I've got a spare toothbrush and everything. You and Sunny are more than welcome. So, how about that drink? I've got a nice bottle of red wine we could open, if that's your fancy."

He's still grinning, and it feels like fireworks are going off in my chest. This is all I want. To ease his burdens. To make him happy.

"Sure," he says, letting out a sigh as well.

I get him set up with a glass of merlot and a bowl of pretzels that he immediately starts nibbling at. It makes me furious to think of him going hungry, but that all stops now. Even if I have to fill his backpack with peanut butter and jelly sandwiches, he's going to have decent food available to him.

More than that, he's going to know that someone gives a *damn* whether or not his tummy is rumbling. I don't care if this is crossing that line I drew in the sand for myself. His wellbeing is all that matters. I can deal with the fallout later.

Even if it is catastrophic.

CHAPTER 5

Xander

I ALWAYS TRY AND BE A GOOD SPORT. IT'S SOMETHING THAT MY mom instilled in me before she passed. There was nothing more important to her than being kind. So even though I'm so worried about not having enough time for school and work and Sunny, I find myself agreeing readily to help Felicia with her increasing number of errands as the date of her sister's wedding gets closer and closer.

I know logically Felicia will never like me, but it's like I'm a masochist who can't stop trying to please her. Like if I carry enough boxes, she'll finally treat me with a little respect. Deep down, however, I know I'm setting myself up for failure. I can't seem to help it, though.

That's why I've found myself with another stack of boxes in my arms as we scurry across town. These ones are filled with gold-painted leaves and twigs for the center-pieces, which I'm sure will be very pretty on the day, but right now I can only think how surprisingly heavy they are.

I've only met her sister, Becky, a couple of times. She seemed even less interested in me than Felicia is, but I think wedding invites are a social status thing, and if the whole

32

family isn't there, it will be a massive insult. So I just need to keep my head down, and it'll all be over soon.

Until then, I need to find a way to tolerate Felicia's increasingly volatile outbursts. I thought it was supposed to be the brides who became unhinged before their weddings, but according to Felicia, Becky would be 'lost without her as her matron of honor.' I try and tell myself that if I wasn't helping, she'd be even more strung out. That takes the sting out of being her pack mule just a little bit.

"Okay, that's the first part of the arrangements sorted," Felicia says, looking at the list on her phone. Of course she's not carrying a single bag or box. "We can pick up the candles now as well, then head to the store to check on the progress of Brigitta's dress."

I wince, knowing how much Brig is going to hate being forced into that frilly monstrosity. But she's a team player. I know she'll put on a brave face, just like Joe and I will. We won't disgrace the family. That's all Dad and Felicia really care about. If that's the only way I can make my father proud of me, then so be it.

We're walking past Paddle Creek's adorable cat café—Toe Beans—when the door bursts open. I automatically stop in shock when I realize that it's Ruben who's suddenly standing in front of us.

Ruben, who's been the nicest anybody has to me in years. Ruben, who cooks me proper meals and frets about how much time I get to study and has let me sleep on his sofa bed three different times now.

Ruben, who I'm pretty sure I love more than ever.

I remember myself in time and smile. The boxes are almost covering my face, but if I'm honest, this is definitely not the most embarrassing situation he's caught me in before.

"Xander!" he cries, sounding genuinely thrilled to see me.

My stupid heart does a flip. *He's just being kind,* I tell myself for the thousandth time. He beams at me for a couple of seconds, then he shakes himself and nods at Felicia. "Mrs. Patterson. Nice to see you again."

I swallow down a snort. After a couple of glasses of that lovely red wine he gave me the first night, I had a full-on rant to him about my stepmom's behavior, and he had several choice things to say about her himself. I'm grateful he's being polite now.

"Oh, Mr. Ward," Felicia says, not even pretending she isn't being fake. "Nice to see you as well. You're not at work?"

I wince at the intended dig. It's so hypocritical because *she* doesn't work. But apparently, that's okay, as she's a wife and mother. However, Ruben should be chained to the garage night and day, so it seems.

He holds up the coffee and paper bag in his hand. "Just grabbing lunch," he says pleasantly without missing a beat. "You look busy." His intended dig is just as obvious to me, and I do my best not to laugh. He means *I* look busy, since I'm the one with all the stuff.

"Well, this wedding won't organize itself," Felicia says with a lofty chuckle. Honestly, I think she's convinced she's coordinating world peace or something. At least it works out well that Felicia loves controlling everything, and Becky seems happy to delegate. It's perfect for them both.

"I'm sure it's going to be a day to remember," Ruben says pleasantly, and I bite my lip to stop myself grinning. Memorable isn't exactly the same as good, and I'm sure he knows that.

Felicia goes out of her way to make me feel powerless, so even though Ruben's subtle jabs are probably going right over her head, they're making me feel extremely seen and supported. I know it's a small gesture, but it means a lot to me.

"I guess we better get going," Felicia says brightly. "Becky and I need to finalize the guest list tonight, and Alexander and I have a lot to do before then."

I marvel that I never hear Becky's fiancé's name mentioned in any of the wedding prep, but that probably just means he has a modicum of sense and is staying out of the way.

Ruben raises his eyebrows. "Oh, if you're finalizing the list, did Joe mention that he wants to bring his new girlfriend?"

"Joe has a new girlfriend?" I ask warmly. He hasn't dated anyone in about a year, so if that's true, I'm happy for him.

Ruben grins. "Yeah, they're pretty serious already. He brought her to his mom's for Christmas."

His expression immediately falls as he realizes what he's said. By the look on Felicia's face, she's definitely slighted that Joe didn't bring this girl to her house over the holidays as well, but then she puts on a big smile, probably sensing a chance to one-up my dad's first wife.

"Of *course* that's fine if she comes to the wedding," she gushes. "I'll text him later and find out this girl's name and menu choices." Her smile drops as she shoots me a pointed look. "You're not bringing anyone, are you?"

Any mirth I was feeling from the interaction with Ruben deflates. "Uh, no," I say in a small voice, shifting the boxes in my arms. Naturally I don't have a plus one, because I'm a sad loser who's only dated a couple of guys in high school and college, and neither of them were serious enough to bring home. Not that they would have been welcome anyway.

I avoid Ruben's eyes, not wanting to see any pity on his face. I'd rather carry on in this silly little fantasy land where he actually kind of likes me, even if it's just as a friend.

"Thank goodness," Felicia says with a relieved laugh. "That will avoid any awkward conversations, at least."

"Awkward?" Ruben repeats with a frown, and I want the ground to swallow me up before Felicia says anything horrible to him. I know he's bigger and older than me, but in that moment, I'd do anything to protect him.

"I guess we'd better get going—" I try and say, but Felicia is already talking over me.

"Yes, awkward," she says firmly. "This is my family, and they are respectable. I'm sure my sister doesn't want anyone waving any rainbow flags and spoiling her big day."

Ruben's eyes narrow as I cringe so badly I think I'm going to fold in on myself. Instead, I try and use the stack of boxes in my arms for cover, peeking out just enough to see Ruben's face.

"You mean she wouldn't want any queer people existing at her wedding," he says.

Felicia rolls her eyes, but she plasters on that fake smile again. "Oh, you know what I mean. It's her big day. It would be impolite to take any of the attention off her."

Or her husband, I think, but decide not to say that out loud. The sooner this conversation's over, the better.

Unfortunately, as much as I love and admire him for it, Ruben is apparently determined to stand his ground. I dread to think how Felicia is going to make this my fault later, but I have faith she will.

"So what if Xander did want to bring a date?" he demands. "Or what if Joe had a new boyfriend instead of a girlfriend?"

"You said Joe was bringing a girl," Felicia says, missing the point entirely.

"He is," Ruben says, running with it. "So what you're saying is that she'd be welcome, but if Xander had a boyfriend, that guy wouldn't be?"

Felicia splutters. "No, not at *all.*" She looks around, checking if anyone is listening to the conversation. I'm sure she cares if other people think she's homophobic much more than actually being homophobic. "I'm just saying that it's good the point is moot because Alexander doesn't have a plus one, so we can avoid any...uh...potentially complicated conversations."

Ruben crosses his arms over his wide chest. "Well, I'm sorry to let you know that Xander does actually have a date that Joe already okayed to come, so your family better get on board with it fast."

"I do?" I utter.

"Is that so?" Felicia says over me with an incredulous laugh. "And who is this mystery man?"

I turn to Ruben, eager to know the answer to that myself. A muscle twitches in his cheek like he's debating what to say. Then he juts his chin up and nods once.

"Me," he says decidedly. "I'm Xander's date."

I drop all the boxes.

CHAPTER 6

Ruben

I THINK I'M GOING TO GIVE UP TRYING TO CONNECT MY BRAIN to my mouth because apparently, where Xander is concerned, logic flies out the window and my heart takes the steering wheel.

"Oh, shit," I cry as all the boxes he's been holding crash onto the sidewalk outside the cat café.

Obviously, I startled him with my ridiculous statement, but I'm not taking it back. Not when his stepmom's jaw is hanging open in shock. I'm not letting her get away with the awful things she was saying.

I place my coffee down along with the bag containing my sandwich. "Here, let me help."

"T-thank you," he stammers as we collect them all up. Luckily, they were all taped shut, so nothing has spilled out. But a couple of them definitely have dented corners, and I don't know how delicate the contents are.

"You're dating?" Felicia states as we stand up again. She's got her hands on her hips, and her eyebrows have disappeared into her perfectly blow-dried hair. "You two?"

I glance at Xander. His expression is shocked, but he gives

me a tiny shrug and a nod, and that's all the encouragement I need to run with this ruse. "Yeah," I say with a smile. I'm still holding half of the boxes, and I give Xander a warm glance. It's easy to pretend this is a big secret that I've been dying to reveal. "You must have noticed he's been coming over to my house a lot lately."

"I just thought he didn't like my cooking," Felicia says with a loud laugh, and I can't tell if she's joking or if she really believes that Xander was trying to piss her off. Knowing that she's been actively refusing to feed him if his timetable hasn't suited her own makes my blood boil, but I manage to stay focused.

"No, ma'am," I say. "We've just been seeing each other for a while since Xander got back into town, and only made things official between us very recently. I hope that won't be too much trouble for you with the guest list, but it would mean a lot if I could accompany him."

She shakes her head. "But...you're almost old enough to be his father?"

I inhale through my nostrils and grit my teeth, but just about manage to keep my cool, otherwise. She can't know that she's insulting my lifestyle as a Daddy, but that's not really what I'm bothered about.

She's commenting on mine and Xander's age gap—which, by the way, is only just over a decade. How about the fact that she's only a couple of years older than her husband's first-born child?

Rather than call her out for being a massive hypocrite, I give her a wink. "Love knows no bounds, wouldn't you say?"

She looks between us, perhaps trying to gauge whether or not we're having her on. Xander is still looking shell-shocked, but after a moment, he gives me such a sweet look it makes my heart melt.

Yeah, I may have just gotten myself in serious trouble, but

I also stood up for him. Hopefully, that's the most important thing right now.

I regard Felicia, wondering if she's going to dig her heels in with the bigotry or stick with manners. It turns out she picks manners. Sort of.

"Right, okay," Felicia says, sounding flustered. "Well…that's fine, then. I'm sure you can both be…respectful on Becky's big day, can't you? Nothing to worry about. I'll, um, add you to the seating arrangements, Mr. Ward. Okay, right. Yes. Well, we better get going, Alexander. We've got a lot to get through today."

"Yeah, sure," he says faintly to her, but throws me a quizzical look.

I nod at him. "We can talk later," I say, leaving it open-ended. Fuck, I really hope I haven't just put my foot in it and made things worse for him. Hopefully, Felicia's fake manners will continue at home, and Xander won't get it in the neck.

"Talking later sounds good," Xander says. He bites his lip and gives me a bashful smile.

Well, at least I'm pretty confident that he's not repulsed at the idea of pretending to date me. But that's all I'll allow myself to think along those lines. Because this *is* just pretend. I won't be taking advantage of him. I'll just have to content myself with hoping I've made him happy with my little stunt.

I guess I'll find out when we talk in a bit.

For now, I hand Xander back the rest of the cardboard boxes, then I watch the two of them hurry on down the street. Eventually, I shake myself and remember to collect my lunch off the ground. The coffee is probably cool by now, but I have more important things to worry about.

The reality of what I've just done is sinking in.

Fuck my life. When I first saw Xander after so many years, I promised myself that I'd stay away to protect us both from this apparently uncontrollable infatuation I've developed in a heartbeat. Then I took him under my wing.

Now I'm pretending to be his boyfriend.

I tuck my sandwich under my arm and use the hand not holding my coffee to fish out my cell phone and call my best friend. He'll be in the office, but his workplace is pretty casual. "Hey, Joe," I cry probably a bit too loudly when he picks up. "Have you got a second, buddy?"

"Uh...yeah," he says, and I can hear the smirk in his voice. "Why are you being a weirdo?"

I exhale, wondering how best to approach this. "Sorry, yeah, I am. Uhh...you know how I agreed to keep an eye out on Xander."

"Yeah," he says slowly. "What's wrong? Is he okay?"

"He's fine," I assure him. "Sorry, I didn't mean to worry you. It's just...well, something got out of hand. With your stepmom."

Joe scoffs, sounding relieved. "Now that I can believe. Do I have to do some groveling on your behalf?" He doesn't sound annoyed at the prospect. Actually, he sounds amused.

I wince. "Well, Felicia said she and her sister are going to be finalizing the table plans for the wedding tonight, so I told her you're going to be bringing Zoe."

"Oh, cool," he says. "In that case, you did me a favor. What are you stressing about?"

I grimace and close my eyes briefly, then decide to spit it out and get it over with.

"So...Felicia was giving Xander shit about being gay and basically saying it was lucky he didn't have a date to bring because her family wouldn't like it. And I sort of...saw red... and said that *I* was his boyfriend and I'd be coming as his plus one."

There's a beat where I seriously wonder if I've just

flushed two decades' worth of friendship down the drain. But then Joe bursts out laughing, and I start to breathe again.

"Oh, man." He chuckles. "That's genius. Actually, I love it. What did Felicia do?"

I snort. "Well, she couldn't be rude, could she? So she told us in so many words that if we behaved then it would be fine. But yeah, I'm pretending to date your brother now. I hope that's not completely out of order."

Joe blows a raspberry. "Nah. I mean, it's all a joke anyway, isn't it? It's about time Xander got some payback on that woman. So long as he's cool with it. Is he?"

I sigh. The garage is looming up ahead, and I'd really like to wrap up this conversation before I get anywhere near being in earshot of my crew. "I think so?" I admit honestly. "I sort of blurted it out mid-conversation with Felicia, so it's not like I got a chance to check or anything."

"Ah, I see," Joe says. "Well, you guys talk it through. If he's up for going along with it, then you have my full support. I'll explain everything to Zoe as well. It can be something to entertain us throughout what I'm sure is going to be a long and painful wedding day."

He's not wrong there. "Yeah, totally," I agree. "Okay, thanks, man. I'll let you know how it goes."

"Talk later," he says cheerfully before hanging up.

I put my phone away and finally take a sip of lukewarm coffee. Guilt gnaws at me, though. I'm still lying to him. He's only okay with this because he thinks it's all a joke.

The way I feel about Xander is anything but funny.

Fuck. It's like I've got a physical ache in my chest when I think about how hurt that woman's comments made him look. I want nothing more than to take every single one of his problems and throw them into the trash. I want to wrap him up in my arms and keep him safe from the rest of the world.

I want him in my bed. I know I could make him feel *sublime.* He wouldn't worry about anything if I were his Daddy. I would love and cherish him the way he deserves.

But that can't happen, and now I'm going to torture myself by having to pretend for a whole day that we're a couple. To have what I so desperately want be so close and yet still completely out of reach might just break my heart.

But for Xander, I'll do it. I'll do anything to protect him.

Even if it means driving myself insane in the process.

CHAPTER 7
Xander

I'VE DECIDED I MUST HAVE SLIPPED INTO A PARALLEL universe. That's the only way I can make sense of what's happening.

Because why else would Ruben Ward be pretending to be my boyfriend otherwise?

I've got to have asked myself that a thousand times since that scene yesterday outside of Toe Beans. I know he was trying to protect me from Felicia's meanness and it's all just a game, but the way he looked at me when he was talking about how we'd fallen in love…

It felt real.

I take a deep breath and finally kill the ignition. I've been sitting outside Ruben's house for a good few minutes now, and Sunny is starting to paw at me from her perch on the passenger seat. "I know, sweetie," I say as I give her some attention. "You want to go into Uncle Ruben's house. We love Uncle Ruben, don't we?"

She wags her tail and gives me a playful yap. She's been cooped up all day, as I've been working, and I feel bad about that like I always do. I walked her around the block before coming here, but she loves Ruben's yard so much I know she'll be happy for the rest of the evening.

It's alarming how quickly this place has come to feel like home—way more than Dad and Felicia's house. But I can't get too comfy. Ruben has been crystal clear this whole time that he's just doing my brother a favor. He doesn't really want to date me or anything. That would be crazy.

I need to get out of the car and get on with the reason for tonight's visit. We're going to work out our fake backstory and make sure that we don't get caught out in a lie at the wedding and embarrass ourselves. We're actors preparing for a role. The best I can hope is that we're still friends as well.

When Ruben called me his friend, it meant *everything* to me.

All I've wanted my whole life was for him to just notice me as more than just Joe's kid brother, that's all. And we have so much more than that now. I can't get greedy and ruin that because this charade has confused the situation.

Still, my heart is pounding, and my mouth is dry as I get out of my car, grab my backpack, then pick Sunny up so I can cuddle her while we approach the door. I'm in ten times more danger now of slipping up and showing Ruben how I really feel, and my already frayed nerves are on edge.

I treasure this relationship we've been able to build. I desperately don't want to spoil it.

I know this attraction is wrong on several different levels. Not only is he my brother's best friend—and Joe has been nothing but nice to me my whole life when he didn't have to be after our dad left his mom for mine. But Ruben is also eleven years older than me.

That's not normal.

I hate—no, I *loathe*—the way my dad has twice traded in his wives for younger models. His and Felicia's age gap has always seriously bothered me. She's basically Joe's age.

Yet here I am, being attracted to men who could almost be old enough to be my dad, just like them. Because Ruben isn't the first guy I've felt this way about. Both my ex-boyfriends were my age, but that was mostly because I was afraid to try for anything else. I've had crushes on loads of older guys and even hooked up with some.

What's wrong with me? I know this isn't right. The last thing I want is to be like my father in any way.

So I have to fight this attraction. I understand why Ruben did what he did by pretending to be my boyfriend. We talked via text for quite some time last night, and I'm actually very touched by how angry he said he got when Felicia was spouting off her double standards. It *is* wrong that Joe's new girlfriend will be welcomed and my hypothetical boyfriend not. It was very chivalrous of him to rescue me like that.

But now that means we have to be convincing as a couple, and tonight we're going to interview each other and build up a fake back story so we can pull this ruse off.

Oh, god. What if we need to hold hands to make it convincing? What if we need to *kiss?*

I put Sunny down on the porch then lean on one of the wooden beams. I don't think I can do this. I can't lie to save my life! Which won't be a problem when it comes to convincing other people we're dating because my attraction is very real. The impossible part will be hiding my true feelings from Ruben. I'm starting to feel dizzy as I struggle to breathe. This is going to ruin everything. I'm going to humiliate myself by revealing this crush I shouldn't even have!

"Hey, hey," Ruben's voice cuts through my panicked fog. I didn't even hear him coming outside. His hand slips over my back. "Xander, what's wrong?"

"I...I..."

He tugs me, and before I know what's happening, he's

wrapped his arms around me, hugging me tightly to his broad, solid chest. "Shhh, it's okay, sweetheart. I'm here."

I cling to him as tears leak from my eyes and my body shakes. Gently he ushers me and Sunny inside and closes the door, giving me some privacy while I have my meltdown. It hits me that this isn't just about the wedding or my feelings for Ruben. This is also about the rejection I'm experiencing from my own supposed family. The stress of working and studying every hour of every day. The fact that I had to move back into a hostile environment and switch schools just so I could keep my beloved dog.

In that moment, everything just seems too much.

"It's okay," Ruben keeps saying as he ushers me into his living room and onto the sofa where I normally sleep. It's folded up now, so we sink onto it, and he encourages me to cuddle up next to him. "It's all right, baby boy. It's okay."

Baby boy? Somewhere between the freak outs, I tuck that name away to cherish later. Gradually I start to calm down, my tears drying up and leaving me feeling numb. "Sorry," I mumble.

Ruben shakes his head. I feel it more than see it where my temple is pressed against his chest. Then he squeezes my hand and rubs the back of it with his thumb. "Don't apologize, sweetheart. You're dealing with so much. I'm surprised you haven't cracked up before now. It's natural. Do you want to talk about it?"

His words are kind, but I still feel ashamed. And I can't confess what started me off just now because that would mean admitting it's my secret feelings for him that have tipped me over the edge.

I don't want to shut him out, though. "I…I don't want to let you down or embarrass you," I say eventually because that's actually true.

He scoffs and rubs my side. "Of course you're not going

to do either of those things. That's not something to even worry about. Is that it? Or are there other things on your mind?"

I groan, his kindness almost feeling painful to me. "So many things," I whisper. "My head feels like it's full of bees. I don't know how to shut it off."

Ruben keeps rubbing my side, and I fret that I've said too much. We still don't really know each other that well, after all. Have I burdened him with too much of my stress?

But when he speaks, he surprises me. "Would it help if I took charge right now and looked after you?"

I blink. I expected some awkward 'bro' advice about how it would get better. I thought maybe he'd offer me a drink or two to relax. I'm not sure what he means by taking charge, but I melt against him at the thought of it. *Yes!* I just want to switch my brain off and not have responsibility for anything, just for a little while.

"Uh," I utter.

Is that okay? He offered, so I guess it is. But it seems like I'd be asking a lot.

"Only if it would help," Ruben says firmly but gently.

I don't know…the way he says it makes me believe that *he* thinks it'll help. And the fact that he's pushing for it tells me this is something he wants to do.

I feel my lip wobble as I look up to him. "Please?" I say in a small voice.

He kisses my forehead, and it's like the whole world just fades away. "You wait here, okay?" he says as he slips off the couch. I miss his warm, solid body immediately, but he encourages me to snuggle up against some throw pillows then pulls a blanket down from the back of the sofa and drapes it over me.

"Has Sunny been walked?" he asks as he brushes my hair back. His touch sends tingles all over my body.

I take a deep breath then let it out, already feeling so much less overwhelmed. "She had a quick one before work," I tell him.

He nods. "All right. How about you close your eyes and try and nap? Sunny and I will go around the block once or twice, and then when I come back, I'll make you some dinner, okay?"

"We have to talk about stuff, though," I protest, feeling the panic creeping in again already.

But he shakes his head and smiles at me. "There's plenty of time for all that. The wedding isn't for a couple of weeks. Right now, we need to take care of you before you actually have a breakdown."

From someone else, that might have been patronizing. But I know that Ruben means it sincerely.

"Why are you being so nice to me?" I murmur, almost afraid of the answer. But he looks at me with such tenderness that all I feel is affection.

"Because you're my friend now, Xander, and I want to do this for you. I like you."

I bite my lip, my heart fluttering. I'm not sure what that really means, but he wouldn't say something like that out of pure loyalty to my brother. He's got to be genuine, right?

"I like you, too," I say quietly.

He strokes my hair a couple more times, and we look into each other's eyes. It's not weird or uncomfortable. In fact, it's almost like he's putting me into a trance.

"Get some rest," he says eventually. "I'll be back soon. You don't have to worry about anything this evening, I promise."

"Okay, Ruben," I say, amazed at how sleepy I feel. Once I hear him take Sunny out of the front door, I think I must doze off immediately because the next thing I realize is that he's gently shaking me awake.

I hum and rub my eyes as the memory of what happened

comes flooding back to me. Before I can feel embarrassed, though, I see Ruben kneeling before me by the couch.

"Hey," he says softly. "I've made you some food if you feel like it, sweetheart?"

I yawn and nod, my tummy growling and reminding me that I am actually quite hungry. When I sit up, I expect him to lead me to the kitchen so we can eat at the dining table. But instead, he's got lap trays here in the living room. On the plate is a portion of macaroni cheese with a side of peas and carrots and beside that is an apple juice box. It kind of looks like a kids' meal, but for some reason that's a good thing to me and—again—not patronizing. It's all in small bite-sized amounts I can manage right now. He's also got a plate of pasta and veggies for himself but with a soda to drink instead.

"Can we eat here?" I ask, not wanting to make assumptions.

He nods. "That was the plan, if you like?"

I nod and sit up properly. Before I can reach for the tray in front of me, he's already handing it to me. "Thank you," I say sincerely.

He smiles and walks around the coffee table so he can sit next to me with his own food. Then he puts the TV on and starts flicking through some movies. I realize they're all animated ones, but the kind grown-ups and kids can enjoy together. Right now, that feels like exactly the level of entertainment my brain can cope with.

"How about this one?" he suggests. "It's a time travel story set in pre-historic times."

I feel my eyes widen. "I love dinosaurs," I say enthusiastically. I've seen this one before as well, so I know it's good and has a happy ending.

He chuckles. "I thought you might from your job."

I nod eagerly as I pick up my fork. "I know it makes me

tired, but I do actually love it there. I was thinking I'd see if I could work there full time once I've finished college so I can keep saving money. There's just something so cool about dinosaurs. They're fascinating. Some are cute, and some are terrifying. But, like…I can enjoy it in a pure way, not like with human bad guys. A T-rex just wants dinner, after all. I can enjoy dinosaurs without worrying if they're ethical or problematic, you know? So much stuff is complicated these days. I don't know," I add with a bit of an embarrassed shrug. I didn't mean to go on a rant about why I like dinosaurs so much because they're easy for my brain to digest sometimes. But…I guess that's the point of everything so far this evening. Ruben has worked out that occasionally my mind needs a break.

"I totally get it," he says with a grin. He presses play and squeezes my knee. "Dinosaurs are very cool," he says like he's assuring me. The funny thing is, it works.

For the next couple of hours, I don't think about my family or my bank balance or my complicated feelings for Ruben. I just eat my dinner and watch the movie, delighted when Ruben also brings us ice cream with whipped cream and sprinkles. When I start to get sleepy again after the movie is done, he encourages me to go brush my teeth. By the time I return, he's set up the sofa bed and made it so that Sunny and I can snuggle down for the night.

I'm not sure what exactly has shifted between us tonight, but it feels almost like a magic spell has fallen. I'm not certain if it will be there in the morning, but I hope so.

I haven't felt like this ever in my life before, and it's all thanks to Ruben.

CHAPTER 8

Ruben

I DRIFT THROUGH WORK THE NEXT DAY, LOSING MYSELF IN OIL changes, tire repairs, and fixing up grinding transmissions. I get the feeling my team sense that something is up, but for once they leave me alone. Well, they don't give me shit, at least. As we get toward the end of the day, Treyvon approaches me and claps me on the shoulder.

"Something troubling you, boss?" he asks, pulling up one of the many wheeled stools we have around the workshop. He lost the lower part of his leg while on his last tour in Afghanistan, so I try and make sure he's never standing on his prosthetic foot any longer than he has to be.

I glance at the wedding ring on his hand. Having another gay guy around the place certainly makes me feel more at ease, but we've never talked much about personal stuff before. However, I'm pretty sure he and his husband, Rick, are into some kind of kink with their boyfriend, Brady. If anyone might understand what I'm going through on some level, it could be him.

Unfortunately, the person I'd typically talk about this kind of stuff with is Joe, but hell will freeze over before I admit to him that his little brother is currently the one doing an absolute number on both my head and my heart. And other body parts, but I'm really trying to be respectful and not think about that too hard. *MUCH!* Too much.

I sigh and wipe my hands on a rag, also grabbing a stool and my coffee to sit with Trey for a minute. "Do you remember the date that wasn't a date?"

He hums. "Was it—in fact—a date?"

I snort. "No, it really wasn't, but…"

"You'd like there to be dates?" he suggests with a knowing grin.

He's not really my type as far as guys go. I've always been attracted to sweet boys, and Trey is definitely a top dog. But I'd be blind not to appreciate how stunningly gorgeous he is with his glowing dark skin, warm eyes, and brilliant smile. Plus, he's just a really decent man. It's no wonder to me that he's got more than one partner.

I snort, then take a mouthful of coffee while I think about my answer. "He's my best buddy's younger brother. Half-brother, but still."

Trey whistles and raises an eyebrow. "Okay, yeah. I see the dilemma."

I hesitate a second, then I decide to trust my gut and confess what else is eating at me. "I'd like to introduce him to my kink as well, but I don't want to scare him."

Trey's eyebrows rise. "Oh, hello. Okay. Well, you're talking to the right person, dude. I get it. That feeling like once that cat's out of the bag it could be the most incredible connection or ruin everything."

"Totally," I say with relief. "You're in the lifestyle?"

"I'm in *a* lifestyle," he says, flashing me his perfect teeth in a way that suggests he's not going to get into too many details right now, but he's not ashamed either. "Do you think you'll scare this young man with it?"

I chew on my lip. "From what I've seen, I think what I'm offering could help him immeasurably. His mental health is fractious, and I think this could give him a lot of peace. I could take care of him in so many different ways."

"Ahhh," Trey says, nodding as realization dawns on his face. "You're a Daddy, aren't you? The real caring kind."

I chuckle. "Is it that obvious?"

He jerks his thumb at his chest. "You're looking at Papa right here," he says. "The beta wolf. Rick and I are kind of more Doms than Daddies, but we totally take care of our boy. If you think this guy could use some Daddying, why not ask him?"

"It's that easy, huh?" I say, and we both laugh.

He claps my knee and gives it a squeeze. "Nope, but what's the alternative? Life is short, man. Carpe diem."

Those words mean a lot coming from someone who very nearly died in combat, and I think about that. What am I really afraid of? If Xander isn't into the idea of being my boy, I'll never know unless I ask. But from what I've seen so far and how easily he slipped into subspace, I think he'd love being a little. He wants to make the bees in his brain stop, and I might just have the perfect way for him to do that.

I exhale, puffing out my cheeks. "I just really like him, you know? But if it goes wrong, it could fuck up the relationship with my best friend as well as with this guy."

Trey gives my knee another squeeze, then lets me go. "Or it could go completely right, and you'll end up with an amazing boyfriend and an amazing best friend."

"That sounds horribly optimistic," I joke.

"It does, doesn't it?" Trey says with a wink, getting back on his feet. "Think about it, man. What's the worst that could happen? You tell him how you feel, and he's not interested. Or you keep quiet and miss out on what could be something incredibly special."

I rub my thumb against the warm coffee mug. "Rejection or regret," I sum up. "Better to live your truth than a lie, though, right?"

He snaps his fingers at me. "I think so, boss."

I nod as he walks away. Okay. I think I'm doing this. And if I am, that means going *all* in.

———

When I get home from work, I do something I haven't done for years.

I go to the kitchen and find the key to the playroom.

I look down at the red racing car keyring and feel a pang —not so much for my ex himself, as we just weren't compatible in the end—but for that lifestyle I thought I'd maybe said goodbye to for good.

Finding a little in somewhere like Paddle Creek seemed like an impossible task. I didn't want to move to a city where the scenes are much bigger, so I'd sort of resigned myself that my Daddy days might be over or at least on a long pause.

Taking a deep breath, I make my way up the stairs to the second bedroom, then unlock it for the first time in years.

It smells stale, and when I turn the lights on, I see the dust floating through the air. I know I should have cleaned it, but I kept telling myself I'd redecorate it, and that never happened. So it's just been neglected.

The twin bed is stripped at least. I got rid of the car-themed bedding to a thrift store not long after the break-up. There are cars, trucks, trains, and even space shuttles everywhere. That was my ex's thing. But in the end, I'm pretty sure he became ashamed of his desires the more serious his job got, and he stopped finding joy in these innocent things.

No wonder I'm anxious about broaching this with

Xander. Ultimately, my ex didn't just reject the lifestyle. He rejected me and some of my core identity.

But I know I was born to be a Daddy just as much as I was born gay. There's a hole in my heart that only heals when I have a sweet soul trusting me to take care of them. Maybe a playroom will be too much for Xander, but my instincts are telling me that he's such a worrier he's going to need to jump in with both feet to see the benefits of what little subspace can do for him.

I realize that I can just offer Xander this as a kind of therapy. It doesn't have to come with a sexual relationship. Although I'd be lying if I said I wasn't interested in him as a man as well as a boy. But if it really came down to it, I could be his Daddy in a purely platonic way. I can support and care for him and give him the space to roam, and that might be enough to help him with his stress and anxiety.

All right, that can be my back-up plan. But I make up my mind there and then that I'm going to give this a chance. First, I'll clean. Then I'll bag up what I can and get rid of the old theme. Because when I redecorate, I know exactly what Xander's little is going to need.

And it's going to be roar-some.

CHAPTER 9

Xander

I WAS WORRIED AFTER THAT NIGHT THAT THINGS MIGHT GET weird between me and Ruben. It was intimate in a way I can't quite put my finger on. I know I was vulnerable with him when I lost my shit and cried, but it was more afterward when he was taking care of me, in retrospect, that I felt more exposed. I remember my mom looking after me like that when I got sick. But to experience it as an adult was kind of strange.

And incredibly freeing.

I woke up the next day feeling rejuvenated. Ruben made me breakfast, then sent me off to college with a proper packed lunch, telling me to text him throughout the day and let him know how I was doing. I gave him a spare key a while ago so that made things easier when he insisted on keeping Sunny and taking her for a long walk while I was out, then taking her back to my house.

I was amazed at how much better I was able to concentrate in class. I was even able to catch up on one of my papers before heading to work, and the time on my shift flew by. It was like I became a fresher, lighter version of myself after just one evening.

I've seen Ruben several times since. He always insists on cooking for me. I think making sure I'm not hungry has become his mission in life, which I have to admit I love. He's walked Sunny a few more times as well. But he didn't go back into full caretaker mode until several days later when I didn't get the grade I wanted on one of my English papers and some guy at work was seriously shitty to me for no real reason that I could work out.

All I had to say to Ruben in my text was that I'd had a terrible day. He immediately asked me to come over so he could look after me again if I wanted.

That was exactly what I wanted. And again, it worked like magic. It's not as if him making me dinner and watching kids' movies is going to cure my anxiety or get me through my degree or whatever. I know that. It's just helping me be so much more at peace with myself, knowing that there's someone out there who cares about me.

Tonight, he's asked me and Sunny to come over, and there was a tone in his voice when he called me that makes me think there's something going on. I don't reckon it's bad, but I don't know what it could be about, either.

We've already talked about our fake back story for the wedding coming up. It wasn't that difficult in the end. We're basically sticking to the truth in that we started hanging out more once I moved back, and things happened from there. He said that I didn't have to do any kind of PDA I didn't want to, and I'm surprised at how natural the whole thing feels, especially after my freakout.

I try not to be nervous as I reach the front porch. I trust Ruben, and there's no need to be anxious when I'm with him. Except I like to envision things before going into them so I can mentally prepare myself and maybe think up some things to say. I'm still so nervous that one day I'm going to misread a situation and cross a line by showing Ruben how I really feel. Hopefully, today is not that day.

"Hey," Ruben cries as he opens the door, sounding slightly breathless. He's grinning at me, like he's excited but also kind of nervous. I've never seen him nervous before. Something's definitely going on.

"Hi," I say, trying not to break out into a sweat. Is he going to tell me he's had enough and wants to stop seeing me? That he doesn't want to pretend to be my boyfriend at the wedding? Oh, god. My mind is already spiraling with the worst possibilities.

Sunny's pulling me inside, though, and Ruben welcomes me with a hug. Okay. Is that a good sign? He could just be being polite. Fuck, I feel sick.

"Is everything okay?" I blurt out as soon as he closes the door. If it's bad news, I'd rather rip the Band-Aid off now.

He exhales, but then he smiles brightly at me. "Sorry, I know I'm being jittery. I didn't mean to freak you out. Everything's fine. Great, actually. I have a surprise for you. I was going to wait until after dinner, but would you like to see it now?"

"A surprise?" I repeat faintly.

If I'm honest, I'm still quite nervous. I know I should be excited, and there's a voice in my head telling me that if he's gone to the trouble of surprising me, then he obviously must care for me and like me in some way. But my insecurities are too noisy, and there's another nasty voice telling me that it's going to be a cake with 'You're such a burden, fuck off out of my life' written on it with icing.

Ruben nods at my question, then removes my backpack from my shoulders. He sets Sunny free and also takes her leash from me, then offers out his hand out for me to slip mine against. I said to him when we discussed the wedding that I'd be comfortable holding hands, but we haven't actually done it yet. I feel like something shifts between us as I slide my palm against his, and he rubs his thumb against my knuckles.

"This way," he says, leading me upstairs.

My heart starts to pound. I sleep downstairs on the sofa bed, and there's a small bathroom down here as well, so I've never really been to the other floor. This feels scarily intimate all of a sudden. As much as my desire for Ruben rages inside me, I'm uncertain if I'm ready for what's about to happen. Or might happen. *Calm down, Xander!*

Ruben takes another deep breath and stops in front of a closed door. Through the other open doors, I can see a bathroom and what looks like his bedroom, so I'm not sure what this could be. Does he have a home office? Does he want me to help him do his taxes?

I'd laugh at the ridiculous train of thought my brain has taken, but I'm too busy practically vibrating with anticipation. What's going on?

"I've made a space for you, Xander," he says. He's still holding my hand, but with the other, he's playing with a key that he's gotten out of his pocket. It's silly, but my heart skips a beat when I see the little pterodactyl keyring attached to it. "It's a way to look after you, like I have been. You know, when I take charge of everything and you don't have to worry about anything at all other than watching TV and eating dinner."

I nod. "I...I love that," I admit shyly. I think I'm feeling that if I don't acknowledge my feelings out loud, it would protect them or something. Admitting how much I enjoyed that time makes it real, and real things can be taken away.

Ruben licks his lips and rubs the back of my hand again. "This is a special way to feel like that, but even more. Almost like a kind of therapy. It's a gift I want to give you, but I understand if it's too much. I just want to show you that you're allowed to let go and be happy."

I glance down at Sunny, who's sitting at my feet. She looks up at me and wags her tail. I don't think I understand what Ruben's saying, but if he wants to keep taking care of me, I'd really, really like that.

"Okay," I say slowly. "That sounds really thoughtful, Ruben. Thank you."

He beams at me, his eyes going glassy. "You're such a sweet boy," he murmurs. Like so many things he says and does, I feel like being called a boy should come across as patronizing. Instead, it gives me a warm glow in my chest. "Do you want to go in?"

I look at the door and nod. "Yes, please."

I'm surprised that I'm already feeling calmer after what Ruben said. Whatever's on the other side, he's obviously put a lot of heart into it. I like the idea of quietening my brain down and letting him take care of me. Maybe it's like an art therapy room? I've heard of things like that.

Ruben smiles then uses the key to unlock the door. He lives alone so I'm unsure why he feels the need for such security, but I have to admit it makes me feel even more special. Whatever's beyond the threshold is just for me and no one else.

He turns the light on, then steps back, letting me go in first with Sunny trotting along by my feet.

My jaw drops.

I'm not sure what I was really expecting, but this is a million times better than I ever could have imagined.

It's a bedroom. Quite a small one, but there's room enough for a twin bed and a chest of drawers. The walls are light blue and the carpet a neutral cream. There's a window on the opposite wall that lets a pretty good amount of light in.

But it's the way the room is decorated that's over-whelming me and getting me choked up.

The bedding is covered in cartoon Tyrannosaurus rexes doing silly things like driving cars and flipping pancakes. The curtains are made of the same material. Fake trailing plants hang along the wall from the ceiling next to the bed. The lamp is a giant dragonfly, and the knobs on the drawers look like tropical flowers. On the wall opposite the bed, there's a sticker design that looks like a fossilized velociraptor. The rug under my feet is a giant leaf, and poking out from the big potted plant in the corner is a herd of brachiosaurus heads. There's even a green dog bed with a fluffy bone toy in it that Sunny immediately runs to sniff.

I'm drawn to the bed, though. On it is a box of brand-new plastic dinosaur toys, a five-hundred-piece puzzle of a creta-ceous landscape, and a coloring book with a pack of pencils. But best of all, there's a triceratops stuffy sitting in front of the pillows that I immediately pick up and hug to my chest.

"What do you think?" Ruben asks, breaking me out of the little trance I've fallen into. I turn to see him leaning against the doorframe, watching me and playing with the small pterodactyl on the key chain.

I try and clear the lump in my throat, but it's no good. "This is all for me?" I manage to rasp. A couple of tears escape my eyes and tumble down my cheeks.

Ruben immediately moves in front of me, brushing the tears away with his thumb. My heart skips a beat and lodges itself in my throat. I don't dare breathe until he retracts his hand. No one's ever done anything like that for me before.

"I hope I didn't go overboard with the dinosaur theme," he says.

"Are you kidding?" I quickly shake my head, hugging the triceratops tighter to me. "It's like work but better and all mine," I gush. "Did you do this so I don't have to sleep on the sofa anymore? Because the sofa was fine, honestly. And I love this, but do you really want me to have my own space in your house?"

This is…a lot. If I allow myself to hope, it almost feels like he's giving me a drawer for my own stuff. Like we're a couple. But he said this was like my therapy room, so maybe not?

Ruben sits on the bed, encouraging me to join him by patting the mattress. I follow him, sitting quite close. "This is somewhere you can be yourself, Xander. Where you can let your inner child out. You don't have to worry about anything while you're in here but coloring or playing or napping or whatever you want to do."

I nibble my lip and look around, feeling a spike of anxiety. He must sense it because he reaches out and squeezes my knee.

"Is it too much?" he asks. "It's okay to say if it is."

"No," I say slowly, shaking my head before looking back at him, trying to untangle my thoughts. "I love it. But…am I…allowed?"

He raises his eyebrows and gives me a little smile. "Allowed to what?"

"I'm an adult," I say hesitantly. "I should be growing up and growing out of these things, not wanting them more."

He sighs, but it's a happy sound. "That's the whole point. That's why it's like therapy. You can let go of all those adult worries and find a headspace where you just have to think about what crayon you want to use next." He juts his head toward a TV I didn't even notice was mounted on the wall at the foot of the bed. "That's got all my streaming services on it, so you can lose yourself in movies or a TV show, too. Whatever you want. This is your space."

I open and close my mouth again. I want what he's offering so badly, but I still have so many questions.

"But you're a mechanic," I blurt out.

Unsurprisingly, he laughs. "Yes, I am," he agrees.

I realize I need to explain myself. "What made you think to do this? *Why* are you doing it?"

He nods and bites his lip as he looks around. "I see. Yeah. This probably feels like it's come completely out of the blue to you. But it's very natural to me. Xander, I'm a Daddy. When I'm in a relationship with someone, I want to take care of them. I like guys who are in touch with their inner boy. It's a kind of kink." He turns and gives me a serious look. "But I'm not expecting anything from you, do you understand? I truly believe that getting into little subspace can help you, and during that time, I'd like to be your Daddy. But it doesn't have to mean anything else."

"Oh," I say, my emotions even more complex now.

That's a lot to take on board. However, I can't help but also get a bit excited. I've heard about Daddies, but I never thought I'd meet one here in Paddle Creek. I haven't given it much thought. However, in this moment, it sounds like such a lovely idea. Like a balm for my soul.

Does Ruben really like me in order to do this for me? Or is this his way of saying he's not actually attracted to me by offering that it doesn't have to be anything more than a kind of therapy?

"Tell me what you're thinking?" he asks, rubbing his thumb against my knee through my jeans. It's reassuring but also kind of arousing.

I puff my cheeks out and hug the stuffy tighter to my chest. Sunny is looking at me from her basket, wagging her tail. I think she likes it in here.

"This place is supposed to help clear my mind, but right now I'm kind of overthinking everything," I admit. To my relief, he chuckles.

"That's fair," he says. "Let's try and break it down a bit. Do you like the idea of this being your room to lose yourself in?"

I nod immediately. "That sounds amazing," I say honestly.

He smiles, looking relieved. "Good. That's the most important thing. We can start there. I guess the next important question is, do you want to keep coming over here and seeing me?"

That one's even easier to answer. I nod vigorously. "Yes, please," I say, almost feeling a little panicky that he's going to take that away. "I love it here, Ruben."

He laughs reassuringly and rubs my knee. "I love having you here, Xander. I love spending time with you and taking care of you. So I suppose the third thing I have to ask is, do you want to keep being friends?" He looks around the wonderful room. "It's becoming a bit more than friends, though, I suppose."

I bite my lip, my heart racing. I've been so afraid of admitting my feelings, but he's given me an opportunity to stick my toe in the water.

Because it sounds like he likes me quite a lot. Maybe even like how I like him.

"A bit more than friends is really okay with me," I say shyly.

He beams at me. "I'd like that a lot," he says.

CHAPTER 10

Ruben

I GRIP ONTO THE KITCHEN COUNTER AND BREATHE DEEPLY. MY head is spinning and my heart is pounding, but I'm trying to tell my body that everything's okay. That went really well. I expected Xander to have questions—as he should. He needs to understand what I'm offering him and how best to explore his newly found little. This won't work unless he truly gives in and lets go.

But the expression on his face just now was dangerous. It fills me with hope.

I think he has feelings for me as well, and role-playing like this will only intensify them, I'm sure.

If I do this, there's no going back. I have to be absolutely sure before I mess around with my best friend's little brother's heart.

Ultimately, there is no fighting it anymore, though. Xander has become my whole world. His happiness is my only purpose. I can't keep lying to myself that we can be merely friends. Even if the relationship doesn't become sexual, I can't deny any longer that Xander has captured my heart and is incredibly special to me. I couldn't imagine dating or hooking up with anyone else now that he's in my life, and I hope he might feel the same.

The thought of him with someone else makes me grip the kitchen counter even tighter, and I have to laugh at myself and take a couple more deep breaths.

"Whoa, there. Calm down," I tell myself. The possessive caveman look is a bit over the top. But the truth is the idea of anyone else laying their hands on him makes me want to break stuff.

Well, it's not like there's anyone sniffing around him, so I can shove that jealousy down because it's not needed and irrelevant. Right now, Xander is here with me, and everything is going great.

I remember I came down here to make him some dinner. I've left him alone to feel comfortable in his space. He's right. It is a *lot* that I've given him his own room in my house when we've only really been hanging out for, like, four to five weeks. But it just feels so right, and I know it has the potential to do him so much good.

For this first evening, I wanted to fully lean into Daddying him and helping him find his little. So I ignore any reservations I had and get out his new dinosaur plate and cutlery that looks like fossils. It's all made from bamboo, which I think is pretty cool. I quickly make myself a sandwich that I wolf down as I make his meal. He's got a PB&J that I cut into triangles, and I also add a little snack cheese, some chips, carrot sticks, and grapes. It's all food he can pick at while he's doing other things, so my hope is that if he's finding his way into little headspace, he won't have to pull himself out of it to eat.

I get a juice box and head upstairs. It's quiet as I approach the playroom, and I hesitate at the threshold before going in and disturbing him.

What I see makes my heart melt.

He's spread the coloring pencils out all over the floor, and is currently concentrating on a picture of a stegosaurus. The tip of his pink tongue is just poking out of his mouth, and his eyebrows are knitted together as he focuses on his work. The puzzle has been tipped out in a different corner, with the pieces still all in a jumble, but I realize that would be easier to work on a hard surface instead of the carpet. I reckon there's space for me to squeeze a small table and chair in here so he can have a desk for things like that.

"Hey, little one," I say softly.

He blinks as he looks up at me, and I can already see his body has so much less tension in it. "Hey, Daddy," he says, then raises his eyebrows as if he surprised himself. But I told him that's what I wanted to be for him, and hearing that word come from his mouth makes my knees weak.

"That's it, good boy," I assure him quickly. "Daddy's got you some dinner if you'd like. You can keep coloring. It's okay."

He looks down at his picture. "Yay. Thank you. I'm having fun."

Pride wells up in me. I had a very strong feeling he had a little in him begging to be let out, but I didn't know he'd surface so quickly.

"That's wonderful. Why don't you keep your plate on the floor? I'll sit on the bed behind you."

"Okay," he says sweetly.

I hand him his food and give a chew to Sunny that she happily starts gnawing on in her basket. Then I perch on the end of the bed just beside Xander. I place my hand on his back, and he sighs and leans into it.

For a while, I rub my thumb against his skin through his T-shirt, watching as he picks at his food and continues to work on the stegosaurus. Then my hand drifts slowly upward, and I begin carding my fingers through his hair.

"Is this all right?" I check with him.

He lets out the sweetest little sigh. "It's lovely, Daddy. Thank you."

Fuck. I was so worried about this, but now it's all happening so naturally. I'm almost afraid it's going to blow up in my face any second now because I just don't have this kind of luck in my love life. Two months ago, Xander was simply Joe's brother, who I hadn't seen in years. Now he's becoming the most important person in my life, and he's falling into little headspace so beautifully it brings a lump to my throat.

I knew I could be his Daddy. My heart is so full.

"Baby boy?" I say tentatively. He hums in response, letting me know to go on. "When you're in here with all your toys and games and stuffies, would you like a different name to help you relax and let go?"

He looks thoughtfully over his shoulder at me. "Can I do that?"

I nod. It's actually very good practice in my experience to name a boy's little. That way they know who they are and what they want at any given time. "Of course you can, sweetheart. Xander is short for Alexander, right?" He nods. "Well, I was thinking when you want to be little, you can be Lally. That's another short name for Alexander."

He bites his lip and thinks a second before grinning at me. "I like Lally," he says happily.

I nod, my heart swelling. "My little Lally," I say fondly, stroking the side of his cheek as he gazes adoringly up at me.

"Am I?" he asks softly.

"Are you what, sweetheart?"

He blushes and casts his eyes down, but he nuzzles his face against my palm. "Am I yours?" he asks, looking back up at me through those impossibly pretty long dark lashes.

I take a breath. Treyvon was so right. You only live once,

and life is short. What's the use if you don't take any risks? Playing it safe never got anyone what they truly desired.

"I'd love you to be mine, sweet boy," I say. "I think you're perfect."

He blushes harder and looks away again, like he doesn't believe that at all. But I'm not taking it back. I'll tell him every day how special he is if he lets me.

I glance over at his plate and am happy that he's eaten most of the food. The juice box is crushed as well, suggesting that it's empty. Satisfied that he's nourished, I caress his cheek and encourage him to look up at me.

"Baby boy, would you like to snuggle with Daddy? You look tired."

"My brain's been working extra hard," he says with a cute little sigh. "It's all mushy."

I chuckle. "I bet it is. How about you come up here and we can lie down for a bit? You can nap if you want or just relax. It's up to you."

He bites his lip and stares at me for a second. "Cuddles with Daddy," he murmurs, sounding awestruck.

I nod. "That's right. Does that sound nice?"

He thinks for a second, then suddenly crawls up onto the bed. I laugh and lie against the wall so he has enough room to snuggle down next to me. He feels so fucking perfect wrapped up in my arms, and I know that I can protect him from anything in that moment. The world can try. But my boy is safe now.

He wriggles against me, his back to my chest and his head nestled against my arm. I marvel at the sight of him, loving how easily he closes his eyes. His trust in me is humbling, and I vow to never, ever abuse it.

He dozes off almost immediately. I watch him breathe for a while before closing my eyes as well. I'm too hyped up to actually fall asleep, but I find a kind of meditative state where

I rest calmly, knowing I'm exactly where I'm supposed to be in the universe.

I know there are consequences to what we're choosing to do here, and I'm going to have to address them at some point. If this carries on, I'm going to have to have a very frank and possibly painful discussion with my best friend. But I can't control that now or ever. All I can do is see where this change in our relationship goes, and if it's something we both want, I'll have to hope that Joe understands that I would never mess around with his brother.

But I might just be starting to fall in love with him a little bit.

I'm not sure how long we lie in the playroom, dozing on and off. But after some time, Xander groans happily and starts fidgeting.

"Are you awake, baby boy?" I whisper in his ear.

I get my answer as he squirms around in my arms until he's facing me. It's breathtaking to see how different he is compared to his usually anxious self. There's a playful glint in his eyes that Lally has brought to the surface.

"Hi, Daddy," he whispers back. Our noses are practically touching, and his breath ghosts over my lips. "You're a good pillow."

"Is that so?" I ask, unable to stop myself from brushing the tip of my nose against his cheek. He smells so sweet, and his body is warm against mine.

"Maybe…?" he says, sounding unsure.

"Maybe what?" I prompt, hoping to give him some confidence.

He licks his lips and looks up at me with his pretty hazel eyes. "Maybe you could be my pillow tonight, too?"

My heart skips a beat. It's been torture whenever he's stayed over on the pullout bed, just knowing he was so close yet still so far away from me. I want him in my bed so badly, but I have to be honest that if that happens, I don't know how much I'll be able to hold back.

If that's what he wants as well, though, I might just die of happiness.

"I'll be your pillow any time you like, sweet boy," I tell him, stroking his hair again and loving how that makes him shiver. "I like you very much, Xander," I say, deliberately using that name so we both know what kind of mindset we're in. I'm not interested in his little right now.

The lust that blazes through his eyes tells me that it's all Xander I'm talking to in this moment. "I like you very much too, Ruben," he says. Then he scrunches up his nose. "Is it weird if I still call you Daddy? I like you being Daddy."

I chuckle. "Of course it is, sweetheart. If you like, when you're Lally, I can be Dada. How does that sound?"

He moans and buries his face against my neck. "Yes, Daddy."

I rub his back, wanting to take this at whatever pace he needs. But when he lifts his head again, his pupils are blown and he's breathing in little needy pants. "Baby boy," I rasp. "It's okay. You're safe with me. I'm here."

He nods ever so slightly, his gaze dropping to my lips. And that's when he closes the couple of inches between us and presses his sweet mouth to mine.

CHAPTER 11
Xander

I'M FREAKING OUT A LOT LESS THAN I THOUGHT I WOULD BE.

It's as if the time I've spent with Ruben has been slowly unlocking a part of me I never knew was there. A more innocent, more confident side of me. And being in this room with him asking to be my Daddy was the final piece of the puzzle.

I know what I want. I think he wants it, too. So I'm not letting my fear hold me back any longer.

I'm pretty sure I've never initiated a kiss in my life. I've always waited for the other guy to make the first move. But Ruben makes me want to be bold. I trust him, and I don't think he'll ever laugh at me in a mean way if I mess up. I'm safe with him.

I can't believe it was only a couple of hours ago that I was on the verge of an anxiety attack. I seriously thought Ruben was getting sick of me, and now here we are.

Kissing on a bed. Technically, *my* bed. Because I somehow now have a whole room of my own in his house.

How is this my life?

His lips are like soft pillows against mine as he presses them so sweetly to my mouth over and over again. It's like he's worshiping me. Normally, I find kisses are messy, urgent preludes to sex. But this feels like something that's happening for its own sake, and I love it. He rubs his hands up and down my back and arms, skimming my hips and thighs.

His crotch is wedged against mine, and I can feel we're both getting a bit excited. However, I don't feel any pressure like I usually would. The regular fear of whether I'm going to do the right thing or be good enough isn't there. Because I know Ruben is going to take care of me.

The bed is pretty small, so I'm not surprised when he nudges me and encourages me to slide off it. What does surprise me is when we're back on our feet. I thought maybe he'd take my hand or keep kissing me. Instead, he scoops me up off the floor. I gasp and automatically wrap my legs around his solid waist. I know he's bigger than me, but I'm not exactly small. No guy has ever picked me up like I'm a damned ragdoll before. It's so *hot.* I throw my arms around him and bury my face against the side of his neck.

"Daddy," I mumble against his deliciously salty skin.

He rubs my back and nuzzles the side of his face against mine. "I'm going to take you to my bed now to cuddle, baby boy. Is that all right?"

All right? Is he crazy? That's only something I've been dreaming about for *years.* I let out a giggle. "Of course, Daddy."

"What's so funny, little one?" he asks warmly as he walks us from the playroom across the hall to his room. Sunny lifts her head to see where we're going, but then snuggles back down, apparently too content to move. I'm glad. I'm not sure exactly what's about to happen, but I think perhaps Ruben and I could do with some privacy.

"Um," I say in response to his question.

I can feel myself blushing. How honest do I want to be? I

mean, I know for sure now that he likes me. We're making out. He's given me my own room in his house, for crying out loud. But do I really want to admit that I've had a crush on him since forever?

I bite my lip as he sets me down on his bed and switches a lamp on. He surprises me again as he kneels in front of me and takes my hands, giving the knuckles on one of them a gentle kiss.

"Is everything okay? We can slow down if you want."

"This is amazing," I say breathlessly. "We don't have to do much more, but I'd really like to keep kissing. I...I like you so much, Ruben."

He beams at me, stroking the backs of my hands. "I like you a lot as well, Xander."

I swallow and shake my head. "I've liked you for a long time. Since before. Years ago."

I'm trembling slightly. Apparently, I can still get nervous around him. His eyebrows shoot up, and I hold my breath.

"Oh, wow," he says reverently. "Baby boy, I'm honored. I always liked you, you know. But it's different now."

I nod in relief, totally understanding. "You were always so nice to me when I was a kid."

It's his turn to shake his head at me. "You're not a kid anymore, Xander. Not right now." He laughs. "I know I'm calling you 'baby boy' and encouraging your inner little out, but that doesn't mean I don't see you as a man as well. A man I'm very attracted to."

My breath hitches. I guess that should be obvious by now, but I really, *really* like hearing it out loud. I've never felt particularly attractive, not even when I had boyfriends. I was always too scrawny, and even had acne for a while when I was a teenager that made me terribly self-conscious.

Ruben makes me feel so special.

"You're, um, ridiculously hot too, just so you know," I tell him, blushing furiously.

He grins up at me with his dark blue eyes, looking pleased as punch. "Is that so?" I nod. "Does that mean I can kiss you more now, gorgeous boy?" I nod again.

My heart races as he leans up to capture my mouth again. Gradually, he eases me back up the bed toward the pillows and crawls over me. I love how much bigger he is than me, and he smells amazing. So masculine, with just a little tang of engine oil and grease. His soft beard scratches against my face, but not in a painful way. I'm certain my skin will get used to it.

Because I definitely want him to kiss me about a million more times after this.

He skims his hand under my T-shirt, brushing my ribs. It tickles, and I laugh, but it's also sensual. Especially when he rubs his thumb against my nipple, making me moan into his mouth.

"Is this okay?" he asks.

I hold back a laugh, but the situation is kind of ridiculous. "Ruben," I say seriously. "I've been fantasizing about you touching me for *years*. Anything you want to do to me, you can."

His lust-blown eyes blaze as he looks down at me. My cock throbs in my jeans, and I squirm against him.

"You're making me feel like a rock star," he mumbles against my lips with a chuckle. "But Daddy's job is to always check in with his baby boy. There's nothing more important than consent."

I groan and cling to his shirt lapels. "Why is that so sexy?" I say, fighting my grin as I keep kissing him.

He nips at my lower lip. "Because you know Daddy's going to take care of you in every way possible," he says in a low rumble.

"Fuck," I rasp.

He caresses the side of my face and looks down at me, his expression serious. "We're going to take this slowly, sweetheart. You've had a lot to take in and process tonight."

I can't help but pout. Perhaps it's the permission I've been given to be childish that lets it out. "Does that mean no orgasms?"

He snorts and drops his head as he laughs. "Naughty boy. Daddy didn't say that. I'll make us feel amazing, and then we're going to get a good night's sleep, all right? I want you in my arms until morning."

My heart aches with happiness. "Okay, Daddy," I whisper. It's amazing how fast that word felt right on my tongue. But I think Ruben has been acting like my Daddy for ages now, so I guess it makes a lot of sense.

I try to quieten down my thoughts as he rolls onto his side to kiss and touch me some more. I keep worrying that I don't deserve this and it can't be real, but then I just think back to my blissful state when I was coloring in my special playroom. Daddy's in charge. I don't need to fret. My troubles can melt away like a puddle on a sunny day. I don't have any responsibilities other than to be desired. Maybe even adored.

When he moves his hands under my T-shirt again, I lift my arms and help him pull it off. My chest is mostly smooth with just a little dark hair between my pecs that runs down past my belly button to my happy trail. However, when he takes his shirt off, I'm delighted to find a furry auburn forest on his broad chest. He's got muscles. I always suspected as much before, but now I can *feel* them. However, he's not cut. There's a lovely cuddly top layer that feels so good as he hugs me tightly to him.

I still need more, and I'm not disappointed when he starts kissing down my chest, running his hands along my flanks, and encouraging me onto my back again. My breaths are shallow as I watch him undo my button and zipper. He locks his gaze with mine as he curls his fingers around the edge, then he starts to pull my jeans and underwear down my legs.

My leaking cock springs free, and I gasp at both the sight as well as at the sensation of the cool air on the wet tip. Ruben doesn't stop until I'm totally naked. He still has his jeans on, though, as he crawls back up my body. I'm trembling with anticipation as he kisses his way along my inner thigh, his large hand splayed across my tummy, keeping me in place. The other he runs over my hip as his mouth finds its way higher, and then…

Oh, *fuck*.

He wraps his fingers around the base of my hard shaft and slides his lips around the top. I buck up into his mouth, but his other hand pushes me back down, and he doesn't even pause a moment. I love how he holds me firmly, reminding me of who's in charge. He's my Daddy, and he's here to take care of me.

I still writhe on the mattress as he pleasures me, his head bobbing down as he sucks and licks my throbbing cock. He moans, showing me how much he's enjoying himself, and that just makes it even hotter. I grab fistfuls of his duvet and bite my lip. I can't peak yet. I've waited so very long for this. I want it to last.

Luckily, Ruben seems to sense my turmoil. He pops off my length and kisses my hip before moving up the bed to capture my mouth. "Good boy," he mumbles against my lips. "So good for Daddy."

I cling to his shoulders, anchoring myself as I thrust my groin up. The denim on his thigh is almost too much for my sensitive cock, but I'm desperate for more friction. I feel like I'm going to vibrate apart.

He chuckles and nuzzles our noses together. "Okay, baby boy. It's okay. Daddy's got you."

He rolls over and quickly kicks off his jeans and underwear as well. I could feel him before, but now I can see his big, juicy dick, and my mouth waters. It has a slight curve to the right, and I can't wait to get it inside my mouth or my hole.

The size of him would mean I'd definitely need at least some prep beforehand, though, and I need him very badly right fucking now. So I'm not disappointed when he climbs back on top of me and lines both our cocks up, wrapping his hand around the lengths to start jerking us off.

I whimper into his mouth as he kisses me hungrily. *"Daddy,"* I murmur between panting breaths.

He groans and moves his hand faster, chasing both our releases. I thrust against him. It's kind of uncoordinated and messy, but it's also perfect.

"I'm close," I warn him.

He nods. "Me too, sweetheart. You're so gorgeous. Come for Daddy."

It's as if he flicks a switch, and my climax rushes over me like a tidal wave. I cry out, tears in my eyes as I explode all over his hand and my stomach. It's not long before he's bellowing as well, spilling long white ropes that streak across me.

I feel claimed, like I've been mounted by a wild animal and now I'm covered in his scent.

Ruben groans and drops down to gather me up in his arms, kissing my mouth and cheeks and neck. I giggle, high from the orgasm and just so happy with life in that moment.

What an evening. And it's not over yet.

I bury my face against the side of his neck again as we cling to one another, catching our breaths. "That was amazing, Daddy," I manage to say eventually.

He hums, kissing the top of my head. "You were perfect, sweet boy. So good. Can Daddy clean you up now?"

I pull away to look at him. I'm usually lucky if the other guy hands me a tissue after we've come, so I'm not sure what he means. But the thought of him taking care of me more sends a thrill down my spine, so I nod and smile shyly.

I should be used to him surprising me by now, but I'm still taken aback when he stands, slips his arms under my knees and back, then *picks me up.* I wrap my arms around his neck as he uses the bridal carry to get me into his en suite. There, he gently places me back on my feet and gets the shower going. There's just enough room for us both in the cubicle, as there's no tub, but I like that we're squished in together.

The water is hot as it cascades over my body. Ruben does everything for me. He washes my hair and body, sneaking in little kisses whenever he can. He even cleans my most intimate areas, which should be sexy, but it's not exactly. It's definitely very personal, and I love it.

I want to share everything with him.

"Daddy," I say in a small voice. He still hears me over the water, though, and he gives me his full attention.

"Yes, baby boy?"

I run my hands up and down his biceps, getting anxious again despite all the wonderful floaty feelings I've just had. "Do you want to do this again?"

He frowns. "Shower?"

I let out a little laugh. "Um, no. Well, yes. I mean, uh…be together."

Oh, dear. Apparently, I've lost the ability to talk. But thankfully he seems to get what I mean. He touches his thumb to my chin to make sure I'm looking at him. The water is hitting our sides, so I can keep my eyes fully open.

"Xander," he says in that serious tone again. "I know it's

complicated with your brother being my best friend, but I'm afraid it's too late. I've fallen head over heels for you. I want you to be mine—only mine. I want to date you and take care of you and make love to you. If that's what you want," he adds on, and I hear the hint of concern in his voice.

That's okay. I can fix that immediately.

"I want that more than anything," I say, not even trying to choke back the sob that escapes my throat. I fling my arms around him, loving how tightly he hugs me back. "I want you to be my Daddy and my boyfriend. I've wanted you for so long."

I blame the post-orgasm release, but I cry on him for a few minutes at least. He doesn't try and do anything except hold me and tell me everything's all right. After a while, I come back to my senses with a few shaky breaths.

He smiles at me, then kisses my mouth gently. "You've got me, sweetheart," he assures me. "We might have a few tricky conversations ahead of us, but this is too important to me to be worrying about that right now. We'll work it all out together. I'm your Daddy, and I'll protect you with all my heart from anything the world throws at you."

I bite my lip, still feeling teary but also so excited. "That sounds amazing," I whisper.

He grins playfully at me. "It's going to be *roar*-some," he says, waggling his eyebrows.

I burst out laughing at the corny joke, but I'm also secretly thrilled that we have our own word. "Roar-some," I agree with a nod.

Ruben shuts off the water and helps me out of the cubicle. I'd have thought I'd be self-conscious being naked around him when we're not in the middle of sexy times, but it feels so natural. I love that he dries me off before seeing to himself, then he leads me back into his bedroom.

"I have another present for you," he says shyly.

I'm curious after all that what could make him bashful. But he opens a drawer and removes a package wrapped in tissue paper with a bow on top. He hands it to me, and I frown.

"You've already gotten me so much," I protest weakly.

He shrugs but looks kind of proud of himself anyway. "You're easy to spoil, baby boy. I wasn't going to give you this unless you liked your earlier surprise. So I hope you'll enjoy this as well."

I carefully rip open the paper and pull out some super soft clothes. My jaw drops as I realize he's bought me pajamas. I usually sleep in my underwear with a T-shirt, but these are full length pants with a matching tee.

And they have sleepy triceratops all over them.

"I love them," I say, my voice thick with emotion. I manage not to cry again, though. I'm happy and overwhelmed by his kindness, but I'm trying really hard to stop feeling like I don't deserve it.

"Can I?" he says with a big smile as he touches the material in my hands.

I nod, almost expecting it this time when he does something extraordinary. I watch as he goes down to his knees, then he helps me step into the pants before getting back up and slipping the T-shirt over my head. Then he moves to the bed and reaches under his pillow to get out shorts and a tee that he quickly slips on.

"Do you want your dino stuffy?" he asks, and I think of the triceratops in my playroom.

I shake my head, though. "Not right now," I say. "But thank you. I just want to cuddle you tonight."

He lets out a happy sigh and comes over to wrap his arms around me. "The feeling is very mutual, baby boy."

That night, I sleep like a log, without a care in the whole wide world.

CHAPTER 12

Ruben

WHEN I STEP INTO O'TOOLE'S, I'M GREETED BY A BLAST OF warm air and a classic Springsteen track playing on the sound system. The weather is definitely getting warmer now that the season's changing, but as it's raining outside, I appreciate getting inside.

I shake myself off like a dog. "Oi," Donna calls out with a smirk. "Unless you want to clean that up, knock it off."

I grin at her and salute. "Sorry, ma'am."

She huffs and rolls her eyes, but I know she's only teasing.

I glance around, and a raised hand catches my eye immediately. Normally I'd order myself a drink first, but I decide to go and say hello instead. Otherwise, it might feel a bit awkward.

"Hey," I say warmly as I make my way over to Treyvon. We've hung out plenty after work with the gang, but I've never made plans to specifically meet up with him. After a few more conversations regarding my love life at work, however, this was his idea. "How's it going?"

I reach the booth and offer my hand for a shake. He's got a good grip and pumps it once before releasing me and

83

turning proudly to the man by his side. "Boss, I'd like you to formally meet my husband, Rick. Rick, this is Ruben."

"I think we met once after a Christmas party, right?" I say as I shake hands with the older gentleman. His grin is playful, but there's something powerful radiating off him as well.

"I'm not sure I'd count it as meeting after the amount of beer you guys had all consumed, but I do remember that, yes." He winks at me. It's true. We don't have fancy parties at Horowitz's. We order Chinese takeout and play stupid games while destroying several kegs. They're not really 'plus one' occasions. "I'm glad to have the opportunity to get to know each other tonight, though."

"Sure," I agree as I slide into the booth opposite them.

Trey smiles and kisses his husband's cheek. I can tell they're holding hands under the table, and my heart warms to see their happiness. The only thing I really know about Rick is that he and Trey met on their last tour. When Trey suffered his almost catastrophic injury, Rick saw out his tour, then left the service with an honorable discharge to marry the man he loved and settle down. Trey tells the story like it's no big deal, but I think it's pretty damned awesome.

"We ordered wine," Rick says, jutting his chin toward the bottle of red that's probably one of the nicest O'Toole's has to offer. They each have a glass, and there's an empty one waiting for me. "But can I get you a beer? Coke?"

I shake my head and lift my hands. "You guys are doing me the favor. I should be getting the drinks."

Trey snorts and waves his fingers in front of his throat. "It's not worth arguing with him, trust me. He's the most stubborn son of a bitch you'll ever meet."

Rick arches an eyebrow in amusement. "Darling, you wound me."

Trey just grins at him like a naughty kid, though. "I'm sure you'll find a way to punish me later."

I laugh, enjoying the casual kinky talk. A lot of my Daddy community has been online, or less frequently, in person at clubs. When Trey suggested we all meet up and chat through some things, I jumped at the chance.

"So that's a yes?" Rick asks. I recognize someone double checking consent when I see it.

"Please, thank you," I say with a nod. I walked here and planned on walking back home. I think I'm going to need a little liquid courage to help fortify myself for this conversation.

Rick has an air of complete confidence about him as he picks up the wine bottle and pours the third glass. I'd guess he was a few years older than me—late thirties or early forties—but he's already got salt-and-pepper through his hair and short beard that really suits him. He's white but tanned, and the crisp shirt he's wearing over his medium frame clings to his well-defined muscles. Together, he and Trey make a very attractive couple. Or two thirds of their throuple, I guess. I haven't heard much about their boyfriend, Brady, but maybe I will tonight.

"Cheers," Rick says, holding up his glass. Trey and I tap ours to his, the sound ringing through the air over the Queen track that's now playing. There are a few dozen people in the pub tonight, but it's not rowdy, so we don't have to shout to be heard. When potentially facing an intimate conversation, I'm glad we won't have to yell.

"So," Rick says pointedly, flashing a million-dollar smile at me. His piercing light blue eyes make me feel exposed in a tingly way. "Trey says things are going well with your new boy?"

I glance around. It's stupid to feel self-conscious. This is a gay bar. It's pretty much a guarantee that everyone in here is going to be queer or an ally. Still, it's not just my privacy I'm protecting. It's Xander's as well, and nothing is more important to me than that.

"Um, yeah," I say, aware of my bashful smile and the blush that creeps onto my face. "Sorry, I don't normally talk about this kind of thing with anyone but my best buddy, but…"

"But he's your boy's older brother," Rick fills in, sharing a knowing glance with Trey, who nods sympathetically.

I shrug and take a sip of the rich wine, already feeling a calming buzz. "Yeah, pretty much. It makes me feel like I'm doing something wrong, which I don't like. I had a lot of that when I first got into kink. There are enough people judging the lifestyle without me shaming myself."

Trey exhales. "Amen to that, dude."

Rick shrugs. "But you're also a decent human being who's worried about upsetting his friend, I get that. In a way, it doesn't have anything to do with the kink, does it? That's all behind closed doors."

I nod and rub my thumb along the stem of my wine glass. "Yeah. I'd just hate for Joe to think I was taking advantage of his brother or anything."

"Are you?" Rick asks bluntly.

I splutter with indignation. "Absolutely fucking not," I hiss.

"Whoa, whoa," Rick says with a laugh, throwing up his hands. "Just checking, big man. That's a pretty convincing answer."

"Sorry," I mumble sheepishly. "I know how fast this has happened between us, and we've kind of gone all in."

"And how's that working out for you?" Trey asks genuinely.

I take a second to let my heart warm as memories flood my mind. It was such a huge gamble redecorating the playroom for Xander, but he absolutely adores it. He's over at my house almost every day now and sleeping there what feels like every other night. As far as sex goes, we're taking it slowly, not moving beyond hand and blow jobs yet. But just being with him is enough, and I can already see him coming out of his shell so much. That anxiety that haunts him so badly is melting away more and more easily.

"Amazing," I say, hearing the awe in my voice. "I took a risk introducing him to the idea of age play before we made any kind of move between us, but he's such a beautiful little boy. Being with him is like magic. I've never felt like this about anyone."

I realize I was looking at my drink as I spoke. I lift my gaze to see them both regarding me tenderly.

"I'm so happy for you, boss," Trey says without any hint of the usual bullshit we sling around at work.

"When you find someone whose needs and desires so perfectly line up with your own," Rick says, "it can be truly magical indeed." He takes Trey's hand again, and they share a loving look.

"Is that how you met your boyfriend? If you don't mind me asking," I add on. I don't want to pry too much into their private life, but both Rick and Trey light up at the question.

"We weren't intending to date anyone else," Trey says enthusiastically. "We were just looking for someone to play with. Our kink can be fun in groups and I like to top more than bottom, so we wanted to make sure we were both happy and satisfied in our marriage."

"We met our sweet baby boy at an event," Rick explains. "We took him home on the Friday, and by the time Tuesday morning rolled around and no one wanted it to end, we realized we had something very special going on indeed."

I grin, understanding that feeling. "I hate when Xander has to leave. I know it's probably early days, but I want to be there for him whenever he needs me, and just love the shit out of him all the time."

The guys laugh with me. Rick bites his lip and nods. "I dunno, man. If your boy needs Daddying, that's often a core necessity. All relationships blossom into something else after the honeymoon phase fades, but that doesn't mean he won't still want all those beautiful things from you."

I try not to think of my ex, but the rejection burns. "My last boy outgrew me and all the childish things that once brought him such joy," I say sadly, but then I roll my eyes. "Well, actually, I think he put his career first and decided he couldn't have what he wanted anymore."

Trey snorts. "That sucks."

Rick shrugs. "Honestly, it does. But that's also a 'him' problem. I'm sorry you had to go through that hurt and loss, but sometimes people aren't in the right place or time for us, and we have to let them go."

I hum, almost wanting to reject his wisdom. But I know he's right. My ex leaving wasn't actually anything to do with me in the end. But I guess I'm still afraid of Xander deciding I'm not enough as well.

Which, quite frankly, is ridiculous. This relationship is in its infancy, and here I am panicking about it ending already.

"I think if you're honest with yourself, you're confident in what you have with Xander," Rick says with a knowing smile. He tops our glasses up, emptying the bottle, then leans back against the slightly cracked green leather seats. "Right?"

I shrug but can't help but grin. "Yeah, probably. If I stop being such a chicken shit."

Rick gives me that wink again, which if I were a sweet little sub or boy, would probably have made me weak at the knees.

"Now," he says with a flirtatious tone, "I'm all for getting drunk, discussing how great being a Daddy is, and swapping salacious sex stories. But!" He holds up a finger. "There's still a thorn in your paw, isn't there, darling?"

I laugh ruefully. "How do I tell my best friend in the whole world that I've fallen hard for his little baby brother?"

Trey opens his mouth, but we're interrupted as Donna comes sauntering up to our table and swipes the empty wine bottle up. "Can I get you gentlemen another?" she asks, fluttering her eyelashes.

We all crack up, which is what she was after. She's one of the least coy people I've ever met in my life.

Rick raises his eyebrows at me and Trey. "I'm up for another if you guys are. I'm buying," he says firmly before I can even hope to argue.

I shake my head and grin. "Sure, why not?"

"Atta boys," Donna says triumphantly. Then she fixes Trey with a raised eyebrow and a gleam in her eyes. "Now, you. When the hell are you gonna take that chopper out of your garage and come out on the road with us?"

I smirk at my colleague. He's certainly been fixing up that bike forever. After wondering at Christmas, I asked around a bit, and Donna is indeed part of a small motorcycle chapter here in Paddle Creek, of all places. But there are a few of them who go out in groups on their bikes regularly, and I can see the appeal. We all need our people to be our true selves with.

"Soon, soon," Trey says, waving his hands and giving her a kilowatt smile. "I need to get my baby road ready."

"You've been saying that for five years, sweetheart," Rick says in a low grumble but with a big playful energy that lets us know he's joking.

Donna wags her finger as she walks off. "Soon, young man," she calls over her shoulder. "That's a promise."

"Anyway, we weren't talking about me," Trey says, shaking his head. "We were talking about you and your best friend. I say…if he's as good a friend as you reckon he is, just rip the Band-Aid off. He might be shocked, but he'll understand."

I groan and rub my forehead. "It's slightly more complicated than that," I confess. "There was this thing with their stepmom where she was being mean to Xander, and I sort of pretended like Xander and I were already dating so I could get invited to her sister's wedding as his plus one."

Trey blinks. "Huh?"

Rick waves at him to shush. "So you were already pretending to date, and now you're actually dating. What's the problem?"

I sigh. "When I told Joe about the ruse, he thought it was hilarious and didn't mind at all because it was fake." I tap the table to emphasize my point. "He specifically said it was okay because it wasn't real."

Rick lifts his eyebrows and hums. "Okay. Be honest now. Is Joe a good guy or a dick you just happen to have known since you were kids and still love out of habit?"

I scowl. "Joe Patterson is one of the best people I've ever met."

Rick smirks at me and waves his hand with a grandiose air. "Rip the Band-Aid off. He'll get over it."

I open and close my mouth, refusing to acknowledge that it could possibly be that simple. Luckily, Donna comes with our next bottle of wine, and there are a few minutes spent on chit-chat and pouring.

"Fine," I say once we're alone again, throwing up my hands. "Maybe I'm using telling Joe as an excuse to not commit to Xander as I'm afraid after what happened to me last time."

Rick raises his glass. "Good boy," he murmurs in a way that actually does make me want to be a good boy.

"Fuck off," I grumble and lift my own glass. "Right. Let's get wasted and talk about sex and sport and cars and shit."

Trey drops his head back to laugh before clinking his glass to ours. "Sounds like a plan. But—hey." He gives me a stern look. "I think this is all going to be fine. It sounds like you have a wonderful thing just getting going. Don't self-sabotage because you're not convinced you deserve to be happy."

"Ouch," I say with a glare, but then I tap my glass back on his and Rick's again. "Okay, cheers to that."

"Cheers," they agree.

Who knows? Maybe it can be as simple as all that, after all.

CHAPTER 13

Xander

"HEY—EARTH TO PATTERSON." I BLINK AND LOOK ACROSS THE library table at my fellow project group members. "You okay there, buddy?"

"Oh, sorry," I say, feeling myself blush.

I definitely zoned out, damn it. It's hard enough transferring for the last semester of my whole degree. Being the new kid and not knowing anyone sucks when it comes to these kinds of activities where the grade is based on everyone's contributions. Now they're going to think I'm some no-good slacker.

Professor Knight assigned the groups, and I was mortified to discover I'd been put with two of the Paddle Creek Panthers' star players as well as one of the Paddle Creek Kittens' cheerleaders. Talk about an all-star lineup and then me, the dunce in the background. I promised myself I wouldn't let my nerves get the best of me, but I spaced out anyway.

Damn this wedding.

"Do you want to go over the reading material again?" the big guy who spoke to me just now asks. I blink again in surprise. I was expecting him to chew me out, not be nice. Marty, I'm pretty sure his name is. He flips his textbook open and frowns as he looks down at the table of contents.

"Oh, no," I say hastily, looking between him and the other guy, Seth. He seems to be in charge of the group, which I appreciate. I'm always better when I'm given guidance, and I really want to nail this presentation. "I know it, I promise. I just...sorry. I've got stupid shit on my mind, but I shouldn't let it interfere with schoolwork. It won't happen again."

The cheerleader scrunches up her nose at me. She's not dressed in her uniform like you see in clichéd high school dramas on TV, but she is wearing an official Kittens purple sweater with ears on the hood. The name emblazoned in teal on the back says 'Zazzle,' so that's what I've been calling her.

"Hey, mental health is super important," she says, squeezing my wrist. "Do you want to talk about it?"

"Oh, n-no," I splutter in horror. "That's—no—I'm fine. Really, I'm sorry. The presentation is what's important. I—"

"Sorry I'm late!" another guy says as he rushes up to our table. He pushes his glasses up his nose and laughs. "I saw Clayton and had to stop to give him half my PB&J. He's in quite a chatty mood today." I'm not sure who Clayton is, but then again, I've hardly gotten to know any of the students here yet, and I probably won't have the chance to before graduation anyway.

If I graduate. I feel like this group project is already a disaster before it's even begun.

I stare at the younger guy, pretty sure he's not in our class. He's definitely not in our presentation group, but all the others beam at him.

"Hey, Gabe!" Zazzle says happily. She jumps up and grabs another chair from a different table. There are a few other people in the library as well, but no one seems to come near us in this corner by the fire escape, and no one appears to object to us moving the furniture.

But I barely notice any of that because this cute, geeky guy leans down, and *both* Seth and Marty—the star fucking football players—kiss him on the cheeks. Both of them.

I realize my mouth is hanging open and quickly snap it shut. The click makes Seth look at me, and I can feel myself blushing again.

"My and Marty's boyfriend is tutoring us. I assume it's okay if he helps?" I can hear the challenge in his voice, and want the ground to swallow me up so I can escape this humiliation.

Fuck. I wasn't judging them! The opposite! I was amazed and intrigued to realize these local legends are not only gay but in a throuple with someone who looks like they should be bullying, not dating. But now I look like an asshole, and I'm not sure how to walk it back.

"I won't overstep," Gabe assures me as he sits down next to me, confusing me even further. "This is obviously your project. I just love this stuff, and the guys said it would be okay to hang out."

"O-of course, of course," I splutter, trying not to panic. I don't want them to hate me. I really don't. "Sorry. I don't know anyone here and I didn't know you guys were, um, seeing each other. That's all. I didn't know if there were any other gay students around."

Seth's expression immediately softens, and Marty rolls his eyes. *"See?"* he says to the group. "This is why this town needs a Pride parade and one of those gay-straight alliances and shit. We need to stick together. Surely Coach Drevin could sort something out?"

Seth chuckles like he's heard this several times before and ruffles Marty's hair. "I hear you, big man." Then he turns back to me. "You're not alone, dude. Trust me."

Zazzle nods enthusiastically. "I swear half the football team *and* cheer squad are queer in some way. It's like this college actively attracts them."

"It helps that Coach is out and proud and doesn't give a fuck," Seth agrees with a cocky smile.

I look between them all. "I had no idea," I say softly. "I just moved here because I had to go live with my family again."

I know I pull a face at the thought of my dad and stepmom, but I didn't really mean to. After all, I spend most of my time with Ruben now, which is a million times better. But with this wedding coming up...

I'm startled when the newcomer, Gabe, reaches over and places his hand over mine, rubbing his thumb sweetly against my skin. "Is your family not supportive?"

The temptation is high to brush it off. These guys don't want to hear about my troubles, even if that's what distracted me from the project in the first place. But there's such pain on Gabe's face that it hurts my heart, and I'm overcome with the urge to share, because I get the feeling that he needs me to as well.

"Uh, no. Not really," I admit. "My dad doesn't really give a shit about me either way, but my stepmom is obsessed with what other people think, and apparently being gay isn't polite or something."

The whole table snorts and scoffs and scowls. "What a Karen," Zazzle grumbles, which makes me smile.

"My family disowned me just before Christmas," Gabe says, his voice wavering. *Oh.* That's heartbreaking. I turn my hand so our fingers can interlace. "It's for the best if they're not going to accept me, but it's still hard."

"I bet," I whisper.

Wow. No one deserves that. At least Felicia hasn't put me out on the street.

"I'm sorry you're going through something similar," Gabe

adds, but I shake my head because my troubles seem like nothing compared to his.

"It's okay," I say, wanting to lighten the mood. "Hopefully, I won't have to live with them much longer. My older brother and younger sister are actually super supportive of me."

I just hope that's still the case with Joe once he discovers that Ruben and I are dating for real, but that's a worry for another day.

"And, um," I add, feeling ridiculously proud, "I have an amazing new boyfriend who's going to come with me to my stepmother's sister's wedding soon."

That gets the completely opposite reaction from everyone. "Fuck yeah!" Marty cries, lifting his hand up so I can give him a high five. It's a bit awkward and unsure on my part, but I do it. Everyone else is beaming at me.

"Ooh, what's he like?" Zazzle asks enthusiastically. "Does he go here? Do we know him?"

"Oh, no," I say quickly. I'm not used to people being interested in my life, but it's kind of fun to be in the spotlight for once. "He's a lot older than me. Like eleven years. He's a mechanic."

"Hello, Daddy," Zazzle purrs salaciously. I splutter, surely going beet red, but that just makes her cackle. "He *is* your Daddy, isn't he?"

My mouth is flapping like a goldfish, and I want the ground to swallow me again. I'm pretty sure, thanks to all the school I've missed, I'm the oldest one at the table by a couple of years, but right now, I definitely feel like the youngest and least experienced one. However, Gabe leans in and whispers in my ear.

"It's okay. I have *two* Daddies."

He leans back and wiggles his eyebrows at me. I glance

between him, Seth, and Marty. "Ohh," I say softly, feeling like I've just been let in on a very exclusive secret.

"So Mr. Mechanic is going to this wedding with you?" Seth asks with raised eyebrows. "Was your stepmom okay with that?"

"Not really," I admit, feeling that knot of anxiety in my tummy again. It's times like this I wish I could have Lulu—my stuffy triceratops—with me. But I know she'll be waiting for me at Ruben's house for all the cuddles. "Felicia okayed it for the sake of appearances I think, but she's been super passive aggressive about it since and keeps threatening me not to make a scene."

"What's her idea of a scene?" Zazzle asks.

I shrug. "Me existing," I guess.

They all make disgusted noises. "You guys go and do anything a hetero couple would do," Seth says firmly. "Hold hands, dance, PG-13 kissing. Don't let *anyone* tell you that you don't belong."

Gabe nods at me. "Eleanor Roosevelt said, 'No one can make you feel inferior without your consent.' It's true."

I raise my eyebrows. "I like that," I say quietly. Then I look around the table, feeling bolstered. "You guys are right. We're not going to do anything scandalous. I shouldn't be afraid."

"Damn right," Marty says with a triumphant grin.

I exhale, feeling a little lightheaded. I can't believe this conversation is actually happening. Are we bonding? Is this me making friends? I'm so bad at it I can't tell. But they all make me feel in this moment like they have my back, at least. I can't wait to tell Ruben all about it.

It puts a few things in sharp relief for me all of a sudden. No, I might not have a perfect, supportive family, but I'm not alone. I have my siblings, who I love so much. I have my bestest girl, Sunny, who will stick with me no matter what, and I'm certainly never going to let her down. Now I have

Ruben, who makes me feel like the center of the universe, and I adore him right back. And I might possibly have just made some friends, or at the very least, acquaintances.

Life could be a good deal worse.

"Thank you," I say shyly. "I feel a lot better."

Zazzle sighs dramatically. "I guess that means we have to get back to this dumb assignment now," she says with a giggle. "I much prefer gossip to schoolwork." She winks at me, and I feel confident enough to smile back.

"So where are you guys at?" Gabe asks, sounding very enthusiastic. He's got to be a freshman, I'm sure. I know I'm a couple of years older than a lot of seniors, but he seems very young to me. His excitement is infectious, though. I wouldn't be stubbornly sticking with getting this degree if I didn't love learning this stuff, and his eagerness reminds me of that.

Seth pulls over one of his notebooks that he was using to divide up the roles for the project and looks down at it. I go to try and sum up where we got to, but I'm distracted as the library doors open, and a striking young woman comes in. She's got very short, bleached blonde afro hair and several visible piercings. She makes a beeline for the desk, but it's been unattended for the whole time we've been sitting here. The woman looks around, then spies us before marching over.

"Hi," she says brightly. I notice that her hands not only have a spectacular lime green manicure with nails that look like talons, but she's also holding a small box with a ribbon on it. "Is, uh, the librarian around?"

Gabe lifts his eyebrows. "Ms. Maude?"

The woman glances around again, then leans in to speak in a hushed tone. "Is there more than one super-hot gothy librarian chick?"

Zazzle snorts. "Nope. Just the one."

The woman nods and straightens up. "Fabulous. Is she here?"

"Not for a while now," Seth admits. "But I'm sure she'll be back soon."

The woman hums. "Can I borrow a pen?" she asks, and Marty offers her his. She flips the little tag over that's attached to the box's ribbon, and scribbles 'From Selena' on it. "If she comes back, can you tell her she has a gift?"

We nod and watch her leave the box on the library reception desk before striding out the door again. There's a beat, then a black cat appears out of nowhere. They sit beside the box, contemplating it for a second before deftly knocking it off onto the floor behind the desk.

Marty guffaws. "Should we pick it up?" I ask, not wanting anyone's gift to end up in the trash.

But the table all looks at me like I'm crazy. "No one goes behind Ms. Maude's desk," Zazzle hisses."

Gabe shakes his head. "I do *not* have time to get turned into a frog today."

Seth shrugs. "If she needs to find it, she can ask her Ouija board for help."

I look around at them, completely unsure if they're pulling my leg or not. But then Marty bursts out laughing, and suddenly we all are, getting scathing glances from the other people around us. I can't blame them, but at the same time, I can't make myself feel all that bad about it, either.

It's so strange for me to feel like I belong anywhere or that I'm being let in on secrets and jokes or anything.

I think of Ruben and all the amazing secrets we have. I want to come clean to Joe as soon as possible, but my playroom is for us alone, and it makes me feel special. The way I call him Daddy might not be shocking to these guys, apparently, but it's precious to me. The way he touches me and brings me such pleasure is all mine, too.

I've been drifting through life for so long, afraid to take up too much space. But now I have a boyfriend, a dog, and even if it's just for today, I have friends.

This is my life and I'm finally starting to love it. I'm not going to make myself smaller again for the sake of this wedding just because Felicia wishes I didn't exist. I'm not going to be obnoxious on someone else's special day, but I'm certainly not going to be ashamed, either.

I'm going to be proud and stand with the man I care so much for. The man I've wanted for years and can now finally call mine, much to my disbelief. And once we get through the day—stressful or not as it may be—I'm going to keep living my life being bigger and bolder. That's a promise I'm making to myself right here and now.

No more hiding. I'm Xander Patterson, and I'm here to stay.

CHAPTER 14

Ruben

DESPITE ALL MY BIG TALK AT O'TOOLE'S THE OTHER NIGHT, I'm stupidly nervous by the time the day of the wedding rolls around. I don't want to mess anything up or make anything uncomfortable for Xander. I don't want Joe to hate me or misunderstand my intentions, and in spite of hearing several quite unpleasant things about the bride and Felicia's family in general, I don't actually want to cause a fuss on anyone's special day, either.

"It's going to be fine," I grumble as I fight with my tie. I've been wrestling with it with the help of my bathroom mirror for a good ten minutes now but to no avail. It still looks stupid.

"Hey, Daddy," Xander says with a soft knock on the door. "Are you okay? We need to leave soon."

I glance at my watch and grimace. What he means is we should have left five minutes ago. It's okay. So long as there's no traffic through town, we should still be fine to get to the church in time. In fact, it'll probably be better not to be awkwardly mingling beforehand. But I don't want to risk anything going wrong out of my control and then us being late. Felicia would definitely act like Xander did it on purpose.

"I'll just leave the tie," I grunt and go to pull it off altogether. But Xander quickly steps forward and places his hands on mine, stilling me.

"Can I have a try?" he asks.

I nod, cross because I'm the one who should be looking after him. But he does that adorable thing he does when he's coloring and sticks the little pink tip of his tongue through his teeth while he's concentrating, and soon enough, the tie is perfectly done.

I lean down and capture his mouth for a kiss, my tension and nerves already feeling better. "Thank you, baby boy," I say against his lips. "You look gorgeous, by the way."

I haven't seen him in a suit before. It's nothing flashy, but he still looks dapper, and I love it. He blushes so prettily and smiles at me. "Thank you, Daddy. I was hoping we could get a nice photo of us all dolled up."

My heart aches. "That's a lovely idea, sweetheart." And it is. But it's also more than that. It's telling me that he's as invested in this relationship as I am. If we take that photo, will he want to show it to people? To put it in a frame? Where? In this house?

Would he consider moving in with me so we'd get to enjoy it together?

I know it's far too early to be suggesting enormous things like that, but it honestly kills me whenever he has to go back to that place where he's unwelcome and rarely fed. I'm aware he has his half-sister, but she's just a kid and in the middle of it all enough as it is. I just know his life would be so much happier and easier if he was here with me.

But a decision like that has to come naturally. As much as I want to be his Daddy twenty-four seven, I'm still acutely aware that he's brand new to this lifestyle. Just because I think it's best for him doesn't mean he won't grow out of it as quickly as he jumped into it. I have to be patient and see how things unfold.

Even if it's destroying me to see his pain and suffering.

But not today. Today I can protect him all I want.

I just have to talk to Joe first and make sure we honestly have his blessing. I can't see myself walking away from Xander in the slightest, but I'm not fucking over my best friend, either. If there's any kind of luck in this world, I'll be able to make him see just how happy his brother makes me.

That he's become my whole universe.

"Okay," I say as we finally start heading downstairs. "Does Sunny have everything she needs?"

Xander's precious girl meets us at the bottom of the stairs with her tail wagging. Xander chews his lip and looks around. "She has food, water, toys, and a couple of puppy pads. But maybe I'll let her out one last time."

I nod. "Good idea," I agree.

I know we're pressed for time, but Sunny's comfort matters more than a ceremony for someone Xander's barely close to at all and whom I've never met. So we take a minute to go out into the back yard with her and encourage her to do her business. When she eventually does pee, she's rewarded with so much attention and enthusiasm from us you'd think she'd just run a marathon. It makes me chuckle, but it doesn't stop me from giving her a treat when we head back inside, either.

We pass by the living room on the way to the front door, and I pause as I spy something on the sofa. "Xander," I say, causing him to pause before he starts putting his shoes on. I pick up Lulu, his dinosaur stuffy, and hold it out. "Would Lally like a quick cuddle before we go?"

"Oh," he says, tears quick to spring to his eyes as he reaches for the triceratops. Ah. I did wonder. He's been putting on a good front this morning, but I suspected he has a lot of stress building up, and I think I was right. "Thank you," he says, resting his cheek on Lulu's head.

I pull him against me for a hug, rubbing his back. "Everything's going to be fine," I assure him. "No matter what happens, you'll have me. All right?"

"Yes, Daddy," he says softly but with enough conviction that I believe he knows what I'm saying is true. "I just hope Joe isn't mad or disappointed with me."

I bite my lip. This one's on me. I could have called, texted, emailed, hell, sent a *carrier pigeon* in the time I've had since we got together. But this is an important conversation that I've convinced myself has to be done in person. I suggested to Joe that we get together a couple of times, but we just weren't able to make it work.

So that means we have to have the talk today, sometime during the wedding, and he doesn't even know it's coming.

I kiss Xander's head. "Joe would never, ever be mad or disappointed with you," I promise him. It's me who'll get the heat if there is any, but I keep that to myself. "He might need a little time to process it, that's all," I add, hoping that's true.

Xander sighs and nods. Then he looks down at Lulu. "I guess we better go," he says unenthusiastically.

"You can bring her in the car with you if you want," I suggest. I don't give a single fuck if anyone sees or judges us, but I understand when he shakes his head after a few moments and places her carefully down on the back of the sofa again where Sunny can't reach her.

"She belongs here," he says confidently. "She'll be waiting for Lally when we get back."

"Exactly," I say before kissing his cheek. "I'm proud of you, baby boy. You can do this. Then, however the day goes, we can come back home and snuggle."

I meant to say 'here,' not 'home.' That implies it's his home as well as mine, which I know is what I want, but I can't push him. Not yet. He smiles sweetly at me, though, apparently not thrown by my slip up at all.

"Can we *naked* snuggle?" he asks, tapping my chest with his finger. I drop my head back and laugh.

I have to say that he's been very patient with my insistence that we take things slowly in bed. Don't get me wrong, there have been plenty of orgasms over the past several weeks, but I've been extremely cautious to keep an eye on him and make sure he's not feeling overwhelmed. He's almost like a wild animal that I'm trying to domesticate. I have to guarantee that he trusts me completely before we throw more sex into the mix, because that always complicates things.

I think we're ready, though.

"Naked snuggling sounds excellent," I promise him with a kiss. "What a lovely thought to get us through the day."

"Agreed," he says with a playful grin.

I check my watch. We really are going to be late now, but fuck it. My time with Xander is far more important. "I guess we better go, sweetheart."

He nods and leans down to say one final farewell to Sunny. "Be a good girl! We'll be back soon."

She wags her tail and follows us to the door but sits on the mat and doesn't try to come with us. "She knows we'll be back," I say with a chuckle before shutting the door and locking it.

We hurry over to my truck and get in. I even gave it a thorough wash for the occasion. I'm not going to embarrass Xander if I can help it.

Right, I guess it's time to face the music, and today, there's more than one conductor.

Let's hope we don't lose the beat.

CHAPTER 15

Xander

I DON'T REGRET THE TIME WE SPENT GETTING READY AT THE house. I needed those last few moments to assure myself that Sunny would be okay, considering my nerves for the day. Logically, I know she's left alone for hours at a time regularly. I don't like it, but she's fine.

Illogically, I keep imagining that the house is going to burn down. My anxiety about the wedding is definitely leaking into worrying needlessly about my dog.

So cuddling Lulu with my Daddy was just what I needed to soothe my anxiety. However, then we hit some traffic through town for whatever reason, making us even later. By the time we reach the church, there's no one else outside, and I'm going out of my mind imagining how Felicia is going to go nuclear at me.

Ruben doesn't say anything as we park. He just grabs my hand as soon as he's locked up his truck, and we sprint to the front doors together.

"Cutting it close," one of the ushers says with a smirk as we rush into the foyer. I hate how Ruben drops my hand, but I understand why. The usher—presumably one of the groom's friends—rolls his eyes and takes a silver flask out of his inside jacket pocket. "Don't worry. Of course she's totally late. Women, am I right?"

Ruben and I both hum noncommittally as the guy takes a drink. I rub my chest and try to stop my heart from hammering. I'm sure if my stepmom has noticed we're late she'll still have plenty to say to me about it. But she's been so utterly absorbed by her matron of honor duties I wouldn't put it past her to not even realize I was missing.

As we sneak into the back of the church, I really hope it's the latter.

I can't see Joe or any of my family before we shuffle into a pew, but I'm assuming they're near the front. I don't notice my knee is jangling until Ruben takes my hand and gently but firmly puts pressure on my leg. I exhale and make myself relax until I stop bouncing.

"Thank you," I mouth to him. There's murmuring chatter drifting through the room, but I still feel like I have to be quiet and not draw any attention to myself.

That being said, when I glance at the woman beside us, she's looking at our hands with a scandalous expression. Shame and dread wash through me, and I try to snatch my hand away. But as fast as lightning, Ruben grips on tight. He smiles at me with such affection, and subtly shakes his head.

You know what? He's right. We're not doing anything wrong. I'm sure loads of other couples are holding hands right now. Why should we be made to feel any different?

I inch closer to my Daddy and rub my thumb against the back of his hand, letting his confidence seep into me.

I don't care what some stranger who I'll never see again thinks of us. I'm only worried about my brother. But hopefully, he'll understand. He has to.

Now that I've got Ruben in my life, I'll do everything I can to fight to keep him.

There's movement at the front of the church that pulls me out of my thoughts. Somebody official looking raises his hands to get the attention of the room. "Ladies and gentlemen," he says in a loud, clear voice that suggests he's done this a lot. The binary greeting rankles me, but it's not unexpected, so I try and forget about it. "Please rise for the bride."

The guests all collectively stand, and then a hush befalls the room before a song starts playing that I'm pretty sure was from a vampire movie about ten years ago.

Felicia is the first to appear at the top of the aisle in a bright pink, clingy dress that certainly shows off her, um, assets. She's got her claws sunk into a terrified groomsman who looks about my age, and I wonder if he's someone's younger brother. She beams and waves as she walks down the center of the room, practically dragging the guy to their destination.

A couple more bridesmaids and groomsmen parade down, then the bride herself appears. Becky's dress is absolutely covered in crystals and ruffles, and her, um, assets are also on full display. She's smiling but also sobbing as she clings to her dad. He's technically my step grandfather, I guess. I only met him once before at a Christmas party where he told Brigitta that she needed to spend less time with her head in book otherwise she'd never get a husband.

She was six.

I look down the aisle to where the groom is standing. Or swaying might be more accurate. I'm pretty sure he's absolutely plastered. His crooked tie and scruffy beard certainly add to my assumption.

Becky's wails of—I assume—happiness piece through the quiet church and make me wince, but luckily we're soon seated and once Felicia hands her a tissue, the crying becomes subtler sniffles. Her make-up is still perfectly intact, though, so kudos to whichever brand she's got on.

I tune out of the ceremony as soon as the minister declares that marriage is a sacred act between a man and a woman. He's clearly making a jab at same-sex couples, so I'm not really interested in anything else he has to say.

It's a pretty long and boring affair with several readings from different people, and they try and make us all sing some hymns I don't know. But eventually, I'm drawn back from my thoughts as Becky's hysterics peak again as they're announced as man and wife.

"I—just—love—you—so—*much!*" she sobs before the dude grabs and kisses her. I can see him shoving his tongue down her throat from all the way in the back here, and yet I was worried about Ruben and me holding hands?

The music starts to play again as they walk back up the aisle to a chorus of cheers. Ruben and I clap good-naturedly. If they're happy, that's all that really matters, right?

The crowd slowly starts to filter out behind the rest of the wedding party. Ruben takes my hand again as we step outside into the spring sunshine. I sigh in relief. Okay, we got through the first part. Just the rest of the day to go.

"Xander!" a familiar voice calls out. I turn to see Joe coming toward us with a wave, and I smile despite my nerves.

"He's not going to hate me," I mutter to myself, but I think Ruben hears as he squeezes my hand.

My brother pushes through the crowd to get to us, and I realize he's holding hands with someone as well. This must be his new girlfriend, Zoe.

Zoe is not what I was expecting. At *all*.

She's Asian, with her dark hair in a short pixie cut. I also spot a couple of purple and lime green highlights. Her ears have several piercings, and there's one in her nose as well. She's got a slim, muscular frame and is wearing a corset with flowing pants and killer heels. Tattoos cover her exposed arms.

She jams her hand out toward me. "You must be Xander," she says happily. "Joe's told me so much about you."

I blink for a second before waking up and taking her hand to shake it. "Uh, yeah, I am," I say before remembering how to talk properly. "It's so nice to meet you."

Personally I think she looks amazing, and obviously she has a strong personality. I'm just worried how everyone else here is going to react to that. It's a *very* white, conservative crowd.

"Likewise," Zoe says before greeting Ruben. "And you're the best friend, I presume?" She winks at us as she also shakes with him. "You make a gorgeous couple."

Part of me flinches, because Joe's obviously told her, and she thinks this is a ruse. But the rest of me takes the compliment and runs with it. We *do* make a gorgeous couple. I'll ask Joe to take that photo for us soon before I can forget. Hopefully, it won't be long before they both also know the truth.

We're interrupted as Felicia comes bustling up to us. "Joe, can you please watch your sister? Your father and I are far too busy."

She shoves a disgruntled looking Brigitta into the middle of our group, and I try not to laugh. But her scowl is quite impressive. If someone has dressed me up like a creepy Victorian doll, though, I'd be pretty mad as well. There are ruffles and lace and fake pearls all over that voluminous disaster of a dress.

"Sure," Joe says convivially, not bothering to ask why our father is too busy. He's probably flirting with one of the twenty-year-old bridesmaids already. Felicia turns to go, but Joe throws his hand up. "Oh, Felicia! I'd love to introduce you to my girlfriend, Zoe. Zoe, this is Felicia. She helped our aunt with so much of the wedding preparations."

Zoe grabs Felicia's hand before she can get away. But my stepmom's face has dropped in shock, and she's clearly judging Zoe at lightning speed from her hair to her tats to her clothes. Not to mention the fact that she's not white.

"It was a beautiful ceremony," Zoe says, sounding pretty sincere. But the way Joe covers his mouth makes me think he's hiding a smirk. "Congratulations to your sister!"

Felicia finally frees her hand as if she had it caught in a vise. Then she looks between me and my brother in mounting horror before apparently realizing she's making that face out loud. She was probably wondering which of her stepsons has brought the more embarrassing date to the wedding. But in a flash, she plasters on a smile and simpers to Zoe.

"So nice to meet you, dear. I'd love to stay and chat, but Rebecca needs me. See you later!"

She rockets away from us like her heels are propelled by jet fuel.

"Rebecca?" I repeat faintly. "Since when is Becky 'Rebecca'?"

Joe snorts and gives his girlfriend an apologetic look. "Sorry, babe. I told you."

Zoe just shrugs, though, a smile still on her face. "That's not half as bad as the sleazy dude loudly betting his buddy just now that I've got a dick tucked away in my pants."

My jaw drops, so embarrassed on behalf of my stepfamily. "I-I'm so sorry," I stutter.

Zoe just winks at me, however. "I could have a magnificent dick down there. They don't know."

"Damn right," Joe says, holding up his fist. Zoe bumps hers against it then they both make an explosion with their fingers.

I glance down at Brigitta. She's just grinning up at Joe's new girlfriend. "I like you," she declares.

"I like you, too," Zoe says. "That's some dress you've got on there."

The scowl returns. "I'm going to burn it later," Brig announces.

Zoe holds up her hand for a high five. "Nice. Although let's do that in a supervised environment, shall we?"

Birgitta slaps their hands together. "I bought safety goggles," she says proudly.

As they discuss further fire safety, Ruben leans over to Joe, and nerves flutter in my belly. "Hey, dude. Can I talk to you for a sec?"

"Sure," Joe says, but then Brigitta drags Zoe away to who knows where, and they vanish almost immediately in the crowd. "Uhh, pause that thought. I better go check they're not digging out the matches *just* yet."

Ruben nods, but Joe has already dashed away. I rub my Daddy's arm. "It's okay," I say softly. "We can tell him later when things calm down."

He hums and smiles at me. I know we both want to let the cat out of the bag sooner rather than later, but another hour or two won't make much of a difference.

We're here as a real couple, and soon all the people that matter will know it.

CHAPTER 16

Ruben

Mercifully, the best man's speech finally comes to an end. The atmosphere in the room is decidedly uncomfortable after the several lewd stories the guy just shared about his supposed best friend. Becky, the bride, laughed shrilly throughout the overly long ordeal, but hardly anyone else did.

I exhale loudly as we're invited to leave our tables and head to the bar while they set up the room for dancing the night away. I ask Xander if he wants to walk around the grounds to grab some air, and he gladly agrees.

It's peaceful outside as the evening draws in. We're at one of the town's only country clubs, and I have to say it's quite a pretty building by the creek, surrounded by trees. We can hear birdsong as we make a lap of the grounds in comfortable silence. I relish holding my boy's hand, feeling his warm skin against mine. On trying days like today, I find it's best to take joy in the little pleasures while you can.

When we make our way back inside, the room has been rearranged, the DJ is getting going, and the bar is busy. As I'm driving, I stick to soda and get Xander a vodka and cherry cola to sip on. I see Zoe lean into Joe to say something, then she heads off in the direction of the restrooms.

"I'll be back in a second," I murmur into Xander's ear.

His eyes go wide, then he follows my gaze. "Oh," he says softly over the noise. The DJ is warning us that the first dance is going to be in a few minutes, and we won't want to miss it. "Do you want me to go with you?" Xander asks.

I shake my head. "I'll be fine," I assure him. I think this is a conversation best had just bud-to-bud. "Why don't you find a seat, and I'll come get you in a minute."

He nods, then glances around before giving me a quick peck on the cheek. I'm so proud of him my heart could burst.

"Good boy," I say softly, loving the glow it brings to his cheeks.

I hurry over to Joe before some aunt or bridesmaid can accost him. He's a good-looking guy, and I get the feeling that a lot of women here don't see Zoe as enough of a reason to stay away. Just as an enthusiastic-looking young lady with what looks like half a peacock stuck in her hair starts making a beeline for him, I get there first and touch his elbow.

He turns away from the wannabe seductress and beams at me. "Hey, man. Having fun?" The girl huffs and changes direction, although I'm sure she'll try again later if she can.

I roll my eyes at his question. "Yeah, tons of fun. Listen, have you got a second?"

"Of course," he says sincerely. "Is something up?"

"Uhh," I say, wondering where I should start now that the moment's come. "I'm going to ask Xander to dance with me," I blurt out.

Joe just grins, though. "Oh, definitely do it. That'll ruffle some feathers. You know, you guys have been doing a very convincing job today."

I swallow. "No," I say slowly, making him frown. "I'm not going to ask him to cause a scene. I'm going to ask him because I want to. Joe, we're not playing games anymore. We never really were. I have…*very* strong feelings for him. I'm certain he feels the same about me."

For a few seconds, Joe continues to stare at me with that frown on his face, obviously trying to understand what I'm saying. "You guys are…" he says faintly, shaking his head.

I try not to panic. "A real couple. I know he's your little brother and you always look out for him, but I want to take care of him, too. Just…in a slightly different way."

"You're really dating?" Joe says, his eyebrows finally lifting. "You…and Xander…are boyfriends?"

I lick my lips before answering. "Yes," I say firmly. I feel like we're so much more than that already, but I don't want to overload my best friend right now.

He blinks and takes a swig of beer. "Wow. I did *not* see that coming. I…that's a big surprise, man. I don't know what to think."

I nod. "I know. I wasn't sure how to tell you. I don't want you to worry. I think the world of him. He's so important to me already."

He arches an eyebrow at me. "So you're saying your intentions toward my brother are pure?"

The moment stretches out as sweat prickles on my brow. "There's no safe way to answer that," I croak eventually.

He barks out a laugh and claps my shoulder. "Wow. Fuck. Dude. This is a lot. I'm going to take a while to process, you know? But…well, if there's anyone I'd trust to take care of the kid, it's you."

I snort, starting to feel relieved. "He's definitely not a kid anymore, Joe."

Joe rubs his chin and nods. "I suppose he isn't, is he? Damn. Well, I know I don't have to tell you not to fuck him over."

I squeeze his arm and look him dead in the eye. "I will treat him like a fucking prince," I promise.

Joe grins and reaches out to squeeze my arm back. "You're a king, buddy, that's for sure. I'm happy for you both. I mean it."

I exhale and laugh shakily. "Thank fuck for that. I've been going gray worrying over telling you."

Joe pulls me in for a hug and slaps my back before releasing me. "Nah, man. I get why, but you're awesome. I can't deny it might be a bit strange." He frowns. "A lot strange. But I'll get used to it. If you guys make each other happy, that's all that matters. It's kind of romantic, I guess, right? Like destiny brought you together or something."

I grin and try not to blush. "Or something," I agree.

"Ladies and gentlemen!" the DJ cries into the microphone. "Please welcome to the floor the new Mr. and Mrs. Bellmont!"

The crowd gathers around the dance floor as Becky drags her new husband to the center. A song by one of those British guys with a guitar starts. It's actually a very sweet number about loving his girl for all time, but rather than swaying back and forth as a couple, Becky is dancing energetically around the groom like some kind of exotic bird's mating ritual. I assume it's something she choreographed, but the only interaction she has with her new husband is when he apparently gets bored and slaps her ass hard, making her stop in shock. He grins as his buddies hoot and holler at him for it. She laughs sheepishly, and they finally start a slow dance, inviting others to join in with them.

Zoe has returned so Joe proudly takes her hand and leads her to the floor. I look around for my boy, not wanting to miss this special opportunity.

His eyes go wide as I approach the table where he's sitting. My heart flutters. I feel like I'm inviting him to prom or something. Not that I would have been able to go with any guy back in my day. That's what makes this so important to me. Even now, people want to stop us from doing something so innocent as having a slow dance together.

I'm not having it.

"May I?" I ask, holding out my hand to him. He's trembling as he places his own hand in mine, and his eyes are glassy when he glances up at me. But he bites his lip and smiles as he stands up, looking pleased as punch.

"I'd love to, Daddy," he whispers.

The song is almost over by the time we reach the dance floor, but the DJ puts another slow number on so the couples can keep having their romantic moment for a little longer. We find a space near the cake that hasn't been cut yet, and I pull my boy against me. I'm holding his hand and have the other arm wrapped around his back. He clings to me and rests his head on my chest. I close my eyes and inhale deeply, loving the scent of his cologne and the warmth of his skin. It's absolutely perfect.

For about thirty seconds.

"What do you guys think you're *doing?*" I blink my eyes open and realize that Felicia has appeared by our side and looks utterly furious.

I feel Xander stiffen in my arms, but I just hold him tighter, silently promising him that I've got this. I'll look after him. "Dancing?" I say, subtly asking what the hell her problem is.

"I told you not to make a scene. People are looking!"

"Yeah," I say dryly. "Because you're making a scene."

She balls up her fists and vibrates. "I invited you as a courtesy to my stepson, but I explicitly told you not to draw attention away from my sister on her special day! Get off this dance floor right now!"

I look around. People are definitely staring now. Joe and

Zoe frown at us from the other side of the floor. "Are you all right?" Joe mouths.

I nod. I don't want him getting dragged into this as well.

"We were just dancing like all these other couples," I say smoothly to Felicia. "We weren't doing anything wrong."

"Let's just go," Xander begs. I don't want to upset him, but I also won't stand for this woman bullying him any longer.

"We have the same right to be here as everyone else," I growl.

Felicia clenches her jaw before spitting out her words. "Why does everything have to be a political statement with you people? This isn't about you! This is about Becky!"

As if summoned, the bride appears with her groom in tow. He's got a large glass of whiskey and has a mulish expression on his face.

"What's going on?" Becky demands.

Felicia throws her hands up in exasperation. I'm feeling strangely calm about the whole thing. I'm sure I'll be furious later that Xander had to go through this, but I'm certainly not embarrassed or contrite. Felicia created this drama, not me.

"They won't leave the floor," she cries out at her sister.

Despite my assurances, Joe and Zoe are making their way over to us. No one is dancing any more. I hug Xander closer to me again.

Becky narrows her eyes at Xander, and my anger surges pretty fast at that. "You're embarrassing your mother," she snaps.

To his absolute credit, Xander bursts out laughing. "She is *not* my mother," he tells her. "And we weren't doing anything wrong. Why should we have to leave?"

"Come on now," the groom says with a roll of his eyes. "No one wants to see you guys being gross. Just take it outside, all right?"

He puts his hand on Xander's shoulder as if to steer him away.

I don't even think. I slap the dude away. "Don't touch him again," I snarl.

There's a beat. Then the guy smashes his glass onto the floor and lunges for me. I jerk backward, bringing Xander with me.

The groom goes sailing into the wedding cake.

The whole thing crashes to the floor with him, leaving him covered in icing. There's a crackle of electric static, and the music suddenly turns off. We're left standing in a moment of silence before Becky's hysterical wail pierces the air.

"You've ruined my whole wedding!" she screeches, pointing a finger at us like a witch casting a curse.

Joe grabs my elbow, and Zoe wraps her arms around Xander protectively. "All they wanted to do was dance," she spits out at Becky and Felicia.

The groom and his buddies are howling with laughter as he rolls around in what's left of the cake. Becky is sobbing uncontrollably. Felicia's mouth is hanging open. It's possible she's gone into a kind of shock.

"Let's get out of here," Joe says wisely.

The four of us hurry out of the room with everyone watching us. Some people are even filming, but I don't care. I'm still trembling with rage that somebody *dared* to try and lay a hand on my baby boy.

"Fuck me," Zoe says with a laugh as we burst out into the night air. "You certainly know how to introduce a girl to your family."

Joe shakes his head. "I've seen wild animals with better manners," he grumbles before squeezing my shoulder. "You okay, dude?"

I nod as I take some deep breaths. The fresh air is helping

me cool off and shake away my fury. "Yeah. We knew they were going to be awful. I just wasn't expecting something like that."

"I was," Xander says with a heavy sigh.

Joe removes his hand from me and claps his brother on the arm instead. "Fuck those assholes," he says with conviction. "Who gives a shit what they think? I only care about you and Brig." He looks at me. "And you too, dude. I'm so happy that you've got each other."

Xander's eyes go like saucers. "You know?"

"I do," Joe affirms.

"And...you're okay with it?" Xander asks.

Joe nods. "More than okay, bro. I'm thrilled for you both."

"Ohh," Zoe says softly and nods. "Yep. I thought I was getting a vibe. Not so fake after all, then?"

I sigh happily and draw Xander to my side again, kissing the top of his head as he wraps his arms around my back. "Not fake at all," I assure them.

There's a commotion from inside the venue, making us all look around. "We should probably get out of here and work on damage control later," Joe says.

I agree. "Catch up tomorrow?" I say to him as we part ways to head to our different cars. He gives me a salute before venturing out into the darkness with Zoe.

I'm still hugging Xander to me as we approach my truck. "Are you okay, little one?"

He looks up at me, then to my surprise, bursts out laughing. "That was pretty hilarious," he says through a big grin.

I laugh too before kissing him on the mouth. "Yeah, it was."

He takes a deep breath and regains some composure. "It was also incredibly romantic how you defended me like that, Daddy. I was so proud to be there with you, even if people got nasty."

I wrap him in my arms and just hold him for a minute by my truck. "I wish I could shield you from anything like that," I admit. "But the least I can do is stand up for you when the world gets cruel. I'll always protect you, sweetheart."

"I know," he murmurs against my chest.

Good. That's all that really matters. His family was never going to respect him anyway. I'm his family now.

I'd like to be his everything if he lets me.

"Let's go home," I say to him. This time I mean it. My home is wherever he is, and right now, I need that to be my bed.

Hopefully, if I get my way, he won't be leaving it for a very long time.

CHAPTER 17

Xander

THE ATMOSPHERE IS CHARGED BETWEEN US AS WE MAKE THE journey back to Ruben's place. I'm definitely still anxious about what fallout I'll have to deal with from Felicia after tonight, but I'm able to push those worries down by focusing on Ruben as he drives.

My knight in shining armor.

I was horrified when my stepmom confronted us on the dance floor. I would have just shrunk away and allowed myself to be humiliated by her. But Ruben stood his ground. Not only that, he stood by *me.* He didn't need to put up with any of that abuse, but he did it because he cares for me. I've never felt so treasured in my entire life.

He's the perfect Daddy.

Sunny is ecstatic to see us when we come through the door, and we look after her first, letting her out into the yard, then getting her some more food. But once she's settled, Ruben takes my hand and wordlessly leads me upstairs.

My heart is hammering in my chest. Something's definitely changed. We've had a lot of sex over the past few weeks, but I have a feeling he's got something more in mind for tonight.

God, I want him inside me so badly.

We don't even make it to the bed before he's cupped his hands around my face and is kissing me passionately. I cling to his shirt and kiss him right back. He looked like a movie star in his suit today, but that doesn't mean I'm not willing to rip it off him if necessary. The adrenaline from the fight was apparently lingering in my body still, and now I'm all amped up again and I need my Daddy to take care of me.

"Want you," I mumble against his lips, attacking his shirt buttons. He chuckles and steadies my hands, though. Oh, no. Have I made a mistake? "What's wrong?" I ask.

He shakes his head. "Absolutely nothing, baby boy. I just want to tell you something." I nod, waiting with bated breath. "Xander, I want to make love to you tonight if that's something you want."

All the air whooshes from my lungs. "Y-yeah," I manage to croak. "Yeah, I want that very, very much, Daddy."

He smiles and kisses my mouth. "I have protection, but I'd rather not use it if we don't have to."

"Me neither," I say. "I went to the clinic a while back and all my results were negative." I might have been a *tiny* bit excited about having sex with him, I'll admit. I basically rushed downtown after that first night and made sure I'd be good to go as soon as the time came.

"That's good, baby," he says, but then he pauses for a second. "I need to tell you that I'm HIV positive. I'm on medication, though, and I'm undetectable. Do you know what that means?"

"Oh," I say, taken aback. But it's only a second before I smile at him. "Yeah. It means your viral load is so low you can't pass it on."

He nods, but he's still looking serious. "I'd understand if you still wanted to use a condom, though."

I let out a nervous laugh and cup my hand to the side of his face. I'm not used to being the one who reassures him. That's typically his job with me. But this is important.

"No, Daddy," I say firmly. "I trust you, and I don't want anything between us. Thank you for telling me, but it doesn't change anything for me. I want..." I take a fortifying breath, bracing myself to talk like I've never talked to anyone before in my life. "I want you inside me. I want to feel every inch of you as you claim me and mark me as yours. I want you to fuck me and fill my hole with your cum."

"Jesus fucking Christ," he hisses before seizing me and kissing my mouth with a fevered, brutal passion. "You are mine, baby boy. All mine. My beautiful, gorgeous, sexy boy."

We stumble backward into the bed before crashing down on top of the mattress. It's easy for us to get our suit jackets off and throw them on the floor. I feel bad wrinkling my nice clothes, but not enough to stop kissing the shit out of my Daddy. I'm sure they'll be okay until morning.

We scramble to undo each other's shirts, but then it's simpler for us to each tackle our own pants and belts and the rest. In no time at all, Ruben is back on top of me, our naked bodies pressed deliciously together as he kisses me hard. I love his solid weight and his cuddly, furry body. He smells of his fancy cologne which he saves for special occasions and a musk that's natural to him. I bury my face against his neck and inhale deeply, letting him fill my lungs.

"You're so gorgeous," he murmurs as he kisses along my jaw and down my neck. "My perfect baby boy. You're precious to me, sweetheart. I was so proud of you tonight. You stood up for yourself and stayed by my side. You're so brave."

The praise washes over me like warm sunshine that I

bask in. I dig my fingers into his back, clinging to him as if he's my life ring. I thrust my hips and rub my cock against his hip, feeling his length against my belly. There's a temptation to get off fast with all my lingering adrenaline, but my Daddy promised me we'd go all the way tonight, and if I can think clearly for a second, I know that's what I want.

"Stay there," Ruben mumbles against my mouth before leaving me lying on my back. He reaches over to his bedside table and gets out a new-looking bottle of lube. My breath hitches. I suppose I am a bit nervous. That's natural when we haven't done this before, right? Mostly, I'm excited. I know no matter what, my Daddy is going to make me feel *so* good.

He wastes no time in pumping a large dollop of shiny gel onto his fingers. He hovers over me as he reaches between my legs and begins rubbing my tight entrance. I hiss at the coolness but try my best to relax for him. His big smile is the reward I get.

"That's it, baby," he says warmly as he gently pushes his middle finger past the ring of muscle. "Let Daddy in. You're already doing so well. So gorgeous for Daddy."

I bite my lip as I look up into his dark blue eyes, trying not to get overwhelmed. He often calls me a good boy and things like that, but this is a lot more than usual. It's like he's bathing me in praise, and my heart aches. After such a stressful day, this is like applying balm on a burn.

"It feels good," I utter as he gets his finger up to the second knuckle. "Want you, Daddy. Need you."

He grins and nuzzles our noses together. "Soon, sweetheart. You're being very patient. Just lie back and relax. Daddy's taking care of you, okay?"

"Okay," I say before kissing him on the mouth.

I also reach down to touch his stunning cock. He likes to make himself come with his hand most of the time. I think he sees that as part of his job. But I'm convincing him more and more that I really like pleasuring him as well. The other day I even talked him into letting me suck him off all the way to completion. I was so smug with myself as I swallowed down as much of his cum as I could, the rest of it dripping messily down my chin.

He makes me bold in ways I could never have dreamed of even just a month or two ago. I guess that's what happens when someone wonderful tells you you're amazing every day of the week.

I jerk him off leisurely as he fingers me and stretches my hole. We kiss insatiably. I'm trembling with desire. It's so long since I had this kind of sex. I just want to submit myself so completely to him.

As desperate for him as I am, I don't want to rush this perfect moment, either. But not long after he's squeezed three digits inside me, he kneels back slightly to take his weight, then uses his free hand to cup the side of my face.

"Do you feel ready?"

I nod eagerly. "Yes, Daddy, please," I beg.

He sighs happily, then reaches for the lube once more. If I do say so myself, I've done a good job of keeping his cock excited while he worked on me, but I'm fine to let him take over now as he spreads extra lube over his length and my hole.

He lines himself up and starts to push his way in. "That's it, baby boy," he says as the fat head forces its way inside. "Deep breath in with Daddy for me." He inhales, and I do the same. When we exhale, he pushes farther in, and it burns a lot less than I was expecting it to.

"Wow," I say softly. I take the initiative and lift my legs to wrap my ankles around his back. I place one hand on his chest above his heart, then cup the other against the side of his face. "Feels so good, Daddy."

He kisses me as he inches farther inside. I love how impossibly full I am, but I still want more.

"You're perfect, sweetheart," he murmurs, sucking and nipping at my neck, licking the pulse point. "You feel amazing. So good for Daddy."

"Yes, yes, yes," I hiss, holding on to his shoulders for dear life.

We begin to rock, him thrusting deeper and deeper inside me, hitting my prostate, and making me wail. I love how strong he is. I feel like I'm being smashed into the mattress in the most loving, caring way. Our pants and grunts fill the air, and his sweat drips down onto me. I feel primal and desperate and so utterly cherished.

"Good boy," he rasps over and over again. "That's it. So perfect. Just like that."

"Daddy," I moan, feeling my climax building. When he wraps his hand around my cock and starts stroking me, it's all over pretty quickly. I'm overwhelmed with sensation, drowning in pleasure. I lurch upward and kiss him hard before dropping back down on the pillow and gasping for air as I start to come all over myself.

"Good boy," he cries, still hammering into me and dragging his hand up and down my cock. "So perfect, that's it. Come for Daddy. Good boy."

It seems like it lasts forever. He wrings every tiny drop from me. When I've finally got nothing left to give, he releases my dick and grabs my hips with both hands so he can really slam into me for the last few thrusts. Then he's dropping his head back and roaring. I can feel him pulsing inside me as he spills his load, filling me up just like I wanted.

"Oh, baby boy, oh," he utters as he gathers me up in his arms, holding me tightly despite the fact that we're covered in sweat and cum and lube. I love that it's messy. Nothing in life is clean and perfect. There are always complications and things to overcome.

But with Ruben by my side, I feel like I can conquer any mountain, survive any challenge.

I hope it never ends.

CHAPTER 18

Ruben

I FEEL LIKE MY WHOLE WORLD LIGHTS UP EVERY TIME I SEE Xander approaching my truck. I'm waiting at the place we've been using for a while whenever I pick him up from college. It's a little parking lot near the science building that usually has spaces free. His face always brightens when he recognizes the truck, and he waves enthusiastically, no matter who's around.

My sweet, special boy.

It's been a couple of weeks since the wedding. I was dreading the consequences of our actions on the dance floor, but things have been surprisingly calm from Camp Felicia. According to Xander, she apologized for raising her voice. Not for being a homophobic piece of work, but we both agreed that any kind of apology was so astonishing that it was best to let it slide. Maybe she realized how unreasonable she was? It seems like the two of them have been living in a strange kind of *détente* ever since.

Honestly, if she had any sense, that's what she would have done all along. Xander doesn't want to rock the boat. He just wants a roof over his head for him and his dog while he finishes out his education. It's taken him so many years to get to this point he's practically racing toward graduation. It won't be long now.

That doesn't mean he's any less busy, but he is marginally less stressed with me feeding him and making sure he's getting enough rest and downtime. The playroom works like magic, I swear. Before, I'd have to get him to eat and watch TV, maybe play some games or go for a walk, and eventually, he'd begin to unwind. Now I open that door and it's like a portal to another realm. Lally just rises to the surface, and Xander can let go of all the things that are troubling him.

Unfortunately, I'm not taking him there just now. He was so exhausted the other night I insisted on picking him up from work and bringing him straight to my place. His car is still at the restaurant. So I'm using my lunch break to play chauffeur and ferry him from college to Dino-Mite. He can drive himself over to my house later. He could get one of the rickety trams that this town is known for, but this way I get to sneak in a little extra time with him, which is always a joy.

He's almost at my car when he freezes and looks panicked down by the wheel on the passenger side. I frown and open my door, leaning out. "Everything okay?" I ask.

He points down at the ground and raises his eyebrows. "There's a...that's a..."

My heart rate spikes, and I quickly lean over the other seat to look through the window.

Then I burst out laughing.

"That's Clayton," I say through my big grin. The raccoon looks up at me. He's got an empty candy bar wrapper clutched in his little paws.

"*That's* Clayton?" Xander repeats, still frozen on the spot. "I thought he was a popular student or something."

I snort, reaching into the bag of snacks I made up for Xander. I brought too many things anyway. "He's harmless," I call out as I pry the lid off a box of apple slices. "People think of him as kind of an unofficial mascot for the school. Hey, bud! You hungry? These are much better than that plastic wrapper." I lean out the window and show him the fruit. His beady eyes go wide, and they follow my hand as I wave the apple slice back and forth. "That's right. Go get it!"

I throw the apple onto a nearby grass shoulder and Clayton immediately goes chasing after it. I select a few more slices and hurl them in the same general direction. The cute little trash panda snatches all of them up before running into the trees.

I wink at Xander. "The coast is clear now."

He laughs nervously and rubs the back of his neck. "Sorry, he just startled me, is all. Next time I'll arm myself with a banana or something."

I chuckle as he finally makes his way over to the truck and opens the back door, chucking in his school bag. He quickly pulls off his jacket and T-shirt so he can pull on his work shirt and the T-rex baseball cap that I secretly love. Once he's changed, he hops into the front seat and automatically leans in for a kiss, which I adore.

"Hey, Daddy."

"Hey, baby boy," I say before starting the ignition. He doesn't have long before his shift starts. "How was class?"

"Great," he says, blushing. "Um, Seth and Marty talked to me again. You know, those football players I told you about."

It's so sweet that he thinks that I don't know who Seth Eisen—the Panthers' star quarterback—is. But what's even sweeter is how proud he is to have made some real friends. I reach over and squeeze his knee before reversing the car out of its space.

"That's great, darling. But I'm not surprised. You're an awesome guy. *Roar*-some, actually."

He rolls his eyes but still laughs at my dumb joke. "I don't know. I've always had such trouble making friends, and these guys are *so* cool and popular. But I think maybe it's because they're like us. Um, you know? They're Daddies to that nice guy Gabe I mentioned. It's a secret, but they kind of guessed you were my Daddy, and he shared. It's cool to have friends with, um, that in common."

I can hear the excitement in his voice, and I rub my thumb against his leg. That's exactly how I felt meeting up with Rick and Trey, although I haven't told him that yet, as I didn't get their permission. Hopefully that's something we can discuss soon, though.

"Absolutely, sweetheart," I say instead, really happy that he's making more of a home here in Paddle Creek. I know he and the other boys will be graduating in a couple of months, but social media is fantastic for keeping in touch with people over distances.

I worry that he might want to move again to get away from his family. But hopefully, this truce with his stepmother is the start of a new chapter for everyone. And he's still very close with his sister, after all.

I just find myself still fretting that he'll disappear from my life overnight like my ex did. But I can't control things like that. I can only live in the present.

"So, your shift finishes at seven, right?" I ask.

He nods as he drinks some water and attacks the sandwich I made him. "I can drive right over to your place?" he suggests.

"Totally. I'll head to your house now, take Sunny for a quick walk, then leave her at my place where she can wait until we both get home."

He swallows his bite and wipes the crumbs off his face before leaning over and kissing my cheek. "You're the absolute best, Daddy," he says.

My heart sings. We just fit together so well. He's thriving

under my care, and doting on him is filling the hole that's been in my heart for years.

I pull into the Dino-Mite parking lot, seeing Xander's banged up car in the corner where it's been for a couple of days. I've already given it a once-over at the shop to make sure it's not going to crash and burn on him any time soon. But if I get my way, I'll sort him out a proper replacement with an excellent safety rating as soon as possible.

"Okay, got what you need?" I check.

He pats his pockets. "Phone, wallet, keys," he calls out as he feels each item there. "I'll let you know when I'm on my way later."

I lean over to meet him halfway for a kiss. "Good boy," I say, my heart full. "Have a great shift. Don't get eaten by a raptor!"

He laughs and rolls his eyes. "The four-year-olds are honestly scarier than any dinosaur, but I still kind of love them."

I tap the visor of his cap, making the felt T-rex teeth quiver. "Because you're a sweetheart," I say before booping his nose. "Go and be roar-some. I'll see you at home."

He waves me off from the lot, then I make my way across town to his family home.

Truthfully, it's feeling more and more natural to think of my place as our home. It's just my gut is telling me that he needs to get through his degree first before I propose any more changes in his life. I really hope he'll think about moving in with me, though.

Apprehension rises within me as I slow down to park in front of the house. I've walked Sunny twice since the disastrous wedding. The first time I let myself in with my key, as no one was in, and the second time Brig was there to open the door when I knocked. I feel like my luck must be running out now, though, and I brace myself as I walk up the driveway.

I don't really trust Felicia's peace. She was so strung out making sure that wedding was perfect, and we were part of a catastrophic scene. But the groom and his friends were apparently of the opinion that it was the funniest thing ever, and Becky changed her tune, saying it was hilarious as well by all accounts. So perhaps Felicia is saving face by not holding a grudge now.

At least outwardly. I'm completely convinced that she'll never, ever forget that transgression for as long as she lives.

I swallow my nerves and ring the bell. Neither I nor Xander did anything wrong that day. If Felicia hates me, I really couldn't care less. She's a terrible person.

I smile at her anyway when she opens the front door. She keeps the screen door closed, I notice. For a second, she looks stunned, then the big fake smile comes out.

"Mr. Ward," she gushes. "What a nice surprise."

I hum and give her a polite smile in return. "Mrs. Patterson, hi. I'm just here to walk Sunny for Xander while he's at work."

She blinks, her smile frozen. "Oh, yes," she says, shaking her head and coming back to life. "That's very kind of you, but Brigitta is out right now taking the dog out for a stroll. So there's no need for you to trouble yourself."

I feel my eyebrows rise. I thought Brig had French club, that's why I offered in the first place. But Xander can barely keep up with his own schedule, let alone his sister's as well, so he probably just made a mistake.

"Oh, okay then," I say convivially, taking a step back from the porch. "Well, see you soon."

"Take care now," she says with even more fake enthusiasm before closing the door. It makes my skin crawl, but I manage to keep my face straight until I'm back in my truck.

I tap my thumb on the steering wheel and frown. Something doesn't feel right, but perhaps it's just because I don't trust Felicia's congeniality to last and I'm waiting for the other shoe to drop any moment now.

Well, I can't do much about it at the moment other than texting Xander to let him know about the change of plans. He'll probably want to swing by here and pick Sunny up before coming to my place. We've both got tomorrow off, and we'll want to make the most of that time together, I'm sure.

There's not much point in me hanging around here, so I decide to drop into Toe Beans and grab a round of coffee for my team. It's a Friday, after all, and they deserve a bit of a treat. The uneasiness lingers with me, even as I leave the Pattersons' house, but hopefully, that will ease once Xander comes over.

Everything is always right with the world as soon as I have my boy in my arms.

CHAPTER 19

Xander

I'VE HAD SUCH A GREAT DAY. SCHOOL IS GOING REALLY WELL, but even better, Seth and Marty invited me to a birthday party that's happening next week for Dukey, one of the football guys. They're going to the town's best gay bar, The Ice Cream Parlor. Actually, it's the only gay bar if you don't include the pub, O'Toole's, which has a totally different vibe, according to Ruben. I've heard so much about Creams, but never been. Now I'll get to go with the actual Paddle Creek Panthers.

I'm still a million miles from being cool, but it's so nice to feel like I have some new friends.

Work was fun as well. I find it tough because I'm so tired all the time, but I do actually love it there. Yeah, the décor is old and cheesy, and sometimes the customers can be real jerks. But often, the kids are so happy and hyper, and I love making their visit memorable, especially when it's their birthday.

But it also makes *me* happy. I hadn't realized it completely until Ruben made me my amazing playroom filled with dinosaurs and prehistoric themed knick-knacks, but all this 'kids' stuff' is what I love. It makes me feel calm and joyful. I think I didn't allow myself to understand that before because I was probably embarrassed, but thanks to Ruben, I now know I don't need to be.

I can enjoy my T-rex hat and my triceratops stuffy and my animated movies, and he still loves me. In fact, I think he loves me even *more* for it.

I'm one lucky boy.

I leave my shift in high spirits. My last table was a particularly lovely family that left cash tips for their server, the host, *and* me. I'm not even put out when I see Ruben's text about needing to pick Sunny up from home. It'll only be a ten-to-fifteen-minute detour, and then I'll have the entire night and day tomorrow to spend with my Daddy.

My wonderful, perfect Daddy.

I keep wondering if this is love. I feel like it might be. Obviously, I've been infatuated with him on and off for years in a way that I thought was love before, but this is different. It's real. He truly *sees* me now.

My heart swells whenever I'm with him or even when I just think about him. No one else has ever allowed me to blossom like he has. My confidence seems to be growing daily, and I'm actually daring to dream about the future. I have purpose to my days and such joy in my life.

All because of one man.

I turn my music up as I drive the now familiar route across town. If I can, I'll thank Brig for giving Sunny an impromptu walk when I'm at the house. If not, I must remember to text her tonight. It was very thoughtful of her. I love how the two of them get along. It's the only reason I still feel comfortable leaving Sunny at the house when Ruben can't have her.

I'll feel bad taking Sunny with me when I go, but my plan is absolutely to move out as soon as I can. I guess once I graduate, I can start working full time and actually start building up some savings for my own place.

Although…I have wondered if Ruben might want me to move in with him.

That's probably *way* too fast. We've only been dating a few months. But I can't help but daydream about it sometimes. Okay, I daydream about it a lot, but no one else needs to know that.

I pull up in the driveway and kill the engine. My dad's car is parked there as well as Felicia's, so I assume everyone is home. I check my watch and figure they'll probably have had dinner with Brig already, but that's fine. Ruben will no doubt have something planned for us.

I don't announce myself as I let myself into the house. I never do. Things generally go smoother if Dad and Felicia can pretend I'm not there. I'll knock on Brig's door, though, once I've got Sunny and am on my way out.

I'm careful to take my shoes off before daring to step onto the carpet, but once my sneakers are off, I pad upstairs, eager to see my baby after a long day away from her.

"Hey, girl," I say as I open my door, but then I immediately freeze.

She's not there. Neither is her basket, any of her toys, her food and water bowl, or the leash I always leave on top of the dresser. The room feels horribly still, and my heart trips over in my chest.

No. No, it's probably totally fine. Brigitta maybe took her into her room after their walk, and for some reason brought all her stuff in there as well. Maybe Felicia was on one of her cleaning kicks and wanted my crap out of her way.

I dash across the hall and bang on my sister's door. "Brig? Are you there?" I ask, trying to keep the panic out of my voice. Everything's *fine*. There's got to be a logical explanation for this.

It feels like forever, but it's probably only twenty seconds before Brig opens the door and looks up from her tablet at me with blinking eyes. "Hey," she says brightly. "What's up?"

I glance into her darkened room and don't see any sign of my dog. I try not to lose my mind immediately. "Uh, do you know where Sunny is?"

Brig frowns at me. "Mom said Ruben picked her up this afternoon?"

"No," I say, shaking my head and starting to feel very sick. I pull out my phone and double check his message. "She told him you'd taken her for a walk, so I came to pick her up now."

Brig turns her tablet off and throws it onto her bed before folding her arms and scrunching her nose up at me. "I never walked her. What's Mom talking about?"

It's like someone pulls the fire alarm inside my chest. I don't think, I just spin around and fling myself down the stairs. "Felicia!" I yell as my feet thunder down the stairs. I'm vaguely aware of Brigitta following me as I head for where the lights are on in the kitchen. "Felicia!"

"What's with all this racket?" she scolds me as I come skidding into the room. She places her hands on her hips and tuts. "Your father is trying to relax in his room."

His man cave, she means. Whatever. I know it's her I need to interrogate. "Where is she?" I gasp.

"Who?" Felicia asks sweetly.

"Sunny!" I yell, my father be damned. "I can't find her or any of her things! What's going on?"

Felicia's smiling as she laughs at me, but it doesn't reach her eyes and there's a cruel ring to the sound. "Oh, I'm surprised you noticed."

"What?" I utter. I can feel Brig lurking in the hall behind me, but I can't really tell more than that, as my focus is so narrowed on my stepmother. "What are you talking about? Noticed what?"

She gives me that mean laugh again, waving her fingers through the air. "You're never here. I told you I wasn't interested in having any pets in my house, but your father insisted I indulge you. I draw the line at neglect, though." She lifts her nose up magnanimously in the air. "The dog was scratching at the door I only just had painted this fall. She clearly needs attention, and you can't be bothered to give it to her."

Her smile is like a shark's.

"So I gave her away."

My entire world tilts on its axis. There's a whistling noise in my ears that drowns everything else out. I think I hear Brig shouting, but I'm not sure.

All I can feel is terror.

My legs suddenly spring to life, and I launch myself at Felicia with a speed that startles both of us. I still have my phone in my hand, but I manage to grab her blouse with both hands and yank her so her shocked face is inches from mine.

"WHERE IS SHE?" I scream through choking sobs. Tears are running down my face, and my entire body feels like it's shaking apart. *"Where is she? Where's my baby? Where's Sunny?!"*

Felica shoves me off, gasping for air, then sneers at me. "Calm the fuck down," she snaps, smoothing down her top. "Honestly, there's no need for hysterics. I found a local woman who fosters. The dog will go to a nice home, and she'll be fine."

"But she's *mine!*" I yell desperately. "She's mine, my responsibility, my family! Tell me where she is *right now!*" My legs give out, and I drop to the floor, my hands bunched against my chest like an attempt to stop myself from losing it completely. "Oh my god, she must be so scared. My little girl. Fuck, fuck, *fuck!*"

"I don't know why you're—" Felicia's face falls, and she looks to the right of me. "Brigitta, what are you doing?"

"Filming you," my sister says quite calmly. "In case we need to go to the police. You just admitted to stealing Xander's dog."

Fury twists through Felicia's face, and she jerks her hand toward her daughter, but then she seems to realize what Brig said about filming her. She withdraws her hand. "That's not what happened, sweetheart," she says with that horrible fake smile of hers. "The dog has gone to someone who can find her a better home where she'll be loved."

"*I* love her!" I cry, horror clawing at every inch of my skin. "Oh my god, I'm never going to see her again. She's going to think I abandoned her—"

I'm yanked from spiraling as Brig pries my phone out of my hand. I'd forgotten it was still there. "You're not abandoning her," she says firmly before smiling sweetly at Felicia. "Because Mom is going to tell us exactly where Sunny is, and then we're going to call Ruben, who can go get her, and then I won't have to call the cops."

I finally take a proper, full breath and look through tear-laden lashes between my half-sister and my stepmom. Brig might still be smiling, but the way she's pointing that camera at Felicia she is definitely *not* fucking around. Felicia's eyes are glued to the phone as well, which is absolutely recording. I can see it on the screen.

Brig holds my own phone in front of my face, and a tiny flash of hope bursts through my chest.

"Tell me the address *right now*, Felicia," I sob, Ruben's number ready to dial. I don't trust myself to drive in this state.

But I'd trust my Daddy with anything in the whole wide world.

I haven't lost Sunny. Not yet.

141

CHAPTER 20
Ruben

I'VE GOT ONIONS AND GROUND BEEF SIZZLING IN A PAN WHEN my phone goes off. It's Xander, and even though I'm surprised he's calling, I grin anyway. It doesn't matter that I'll be seeing my baby any minute now. I'm always excited to hear from him as well.

"Hey, gorgeous," I say as I pick up. "Are you on your way?"

"Ruben!" he cries through the phone. I drop the spatula as my heart threatens to stop.

"What is it, baby? What's wrong?"

There are a couple of horrendous sobs that hit me like bullets, but then he's able to speak again. "Felicia gave Sunny away."

My blood turns to ice. "She did *what?*"

That woman's faint voice travels down the line. "I did no such th—"

"Quit it, Mom!" Brigitta snaps, sounding much closer to my boy. "It's okay, Xander. Tell Ruben."

"She gave me the address," Xander manages to say. He sounds absolutely wrecked, and my urge to punch things only increases. "She said this woman fosters dogs until they can find forever homes. But *I* was supposed to be Sunny's forever home! She's going to end up in a shelter again, and I—"

"Hey, Xander," I bark loudly, making him stop. "Listen to me, okay? That's not going to happen. What's the address? I can go get her right now."

Brig must be listening in, because she pipes up with a gentle "I told you so." I realize that's why he called me.

My baby needs me to save him.

I'm already running to the front door to grab my keys. "Thank you," Xander rasps, his voice hoarse and broken from crying. "It's near the swimming pool. Thank you, Ruben, thank you."

He rattles off the address. I only just remember to run back to the kitchen and turn off the stove, but then I'm dashing right back to my open door and the truck. "It's going to be okay, baby," I promise him as I lock the door and then bolt across the drive. "I'm going to hang up now so I can drive faster. Are you okay? Can you stay with your sister?"

He whimpers, and I can imagine him nodding. "Yes, Daddy," he whispers. I don't care who hears. I am his Daddy, and I'm going to fix this dognapping even if I have to go all Liam Neeson in this whole town.

Starting with Felicia fucking Patterson.

"I'll call you as soon as I get there," I promise.

"Okay, okay," he says breathlessly.

"Thank you, Ruben," Brigitta calls out. I know she's only a little girl, but as I end the call, I'm really glad she's there with my boy. Maybe her presence can keep Felicia from doing anything else heinous.

I barely stick to the speed limit as I let my GPS guide me to the house. My heart is hammering in my chest. I have no idea what I'm walking into. All I know is I can't leave without Sunny.

It's an ordinary looking residential street with two-story detached houses. Dusk is settling, but the streetlights have already come on, so I'm more easily able to hunt for the correct number. Thankfully, there's room to park outside, and I take that as a good omen. I jog up the path, noting the neatly trimmed lawn and a few cute stone ornaments nestled in the flower beds. There's a sign on the porch saying "Warning! A lot of very spoiled dogs live here!"

Well, at least it looks like I'm in the right place.

Taking a deep breath, I waste no time ringing the doorbell. I hear a great deal of barking from what has to be several dogs, then a muffled voice telling them that everything's okay.

A brunette woman in her forties or fifties smiles at me as she opens the door a crack. She's not wearing any make-up, and her jeans are definitely made for function over fashion. My instinct is to warm to her, but that depends on how the next few minutes go. She's using her legs to hold back a couple of quite large dogs who seem very eager to meet me.

"Hi?" she greets me.

I nod back at her. "Evening, ma'am," I say, keeping my voice steady. "I'm sorry to disturb you, but I'm hoping you can help me. It's regarding a dog I believe you took in today."

"Uh, sure," she says, her expression wavering slightly. "All my adoptions go through the official Perfect Paws website, though."

I shake my head. I knew it was going to be my word against Felicia's. I just pray that this woman is a decent soul.

"I'm not here to adopt," I say calmly but firmly. "There's been a terrible mistake. My boyfriend's stepmother took his dog without his permission and gave her to you. Her name is Sunny, and she's small, fluffy, and a sort of brown and caramel color. He's incredibly anxious to get her back."

The woman looks very confused now. Her brow is knitted, and she's biting her lip as she wraps her cardigan tighter around herself. "There was a woman here earlier, yes. She said she found me online and that she needed to rehome the family dog fast as her daughter has become allergic."

I shake my head. "Completely untrue. I'm afraid this woman was acting out of pure spite." I get my phone out. "I promised my boyfriend I'd call him when I got here, but maybe some photos of him and Sunny might help? We can video call him afterward so you can see it's the same person."

It's easy to find what I'm looking for. Xander's Instagram is pretty much only pictures of him and Sunny. The only one that isn't is the most recent one of me and him from the wedding in our suits. My heart aches, but I skip past it to the ones we need.

"Oh," says the woman. Her eyes go wide as she looks at all the images. "That certainly could be the little girl I took in earlier. But that would mean…" She covers her mouth and switches her gaze upward to look at me. "Did I help this woman *steal* your boyfriend's dog?"

I can't help the flares of hope and relief that surge through me. That sounds like she believes me.

I shake my head, feeling her pain. How was she to know? "It's okay. We can fix it. But I'd really like to see Sunny now, if that's okay?"

"Of course, of course," the lady splutters, then waves at the dogs who are dancing behind her legs still. "Okay, back it up, guys," she says in a commanding tone that has them all doing as they're told so I can step inside. "I've got her in the dining room at the back with some of the quieter ones. She was trembling. Oh…the poor baby. If only I'd known."

"Honestly, it's not your fault," I assure her. There are several dogs of all sizes circling around me and sniffing, but they mostly behave themselves. "My boyfriend was distraught when he found out, though, so I'd like to reunite them as fast as I can."

"Just in here," the woman says, heading toward a closed door. "I'm Katrina, by the way. Urgh, this is why I usually let the company sort the adoptions, but that woman said it was urgent. I can't believe anyone would do such a thing."

"I can," I grumble under my breath. I knew Felicia hadn't gotten over that incident at the wedding, but this is low, even for her.

We make our way into the room without letting any of the dogs on either side in or out. I see Sunny immediately. She's curled up in her bed behind the dining table, looking smaller than usual. Next to her is a box, and even at a glance, I can see her familiar purple squeaky penguin and a bag of her brand of kibble. She wags her tail timidly, but as I crouch down, she obviously realizes it's me and jumps up, barking and quivering as she scrabbles over the floor to get to me.

My heart almost breaks with relief. "Hey! Hey, girl," I coo, stroking her and letting her lick my hand. "It's okay. Uncle Ruben's here. We're going to get you back to your daddy now." I use my free hand to video call Xander, not surprised when he picks up immediately.

"Ruben?" he cries.

I've got a lump in my throat as I smile at him and hug Sunny to my chest so he can see her. "Everything's okay, sweetheart. Look."

He makes a keening noise like a wounded animal. "Sunny! Sunny!" he shouts. Poor Sunny looks around in confusion, obviously hearing his voice but not understanding where he is. "Please! Oh please! Tell her I'll pay her anything! I'll do anything! Don't leave her there!"

"Hey, hey, shhhh," I tell him, looking into his eyes through the screen. The pain in them makes me so furious, but I don't need to get mad because I know everything's going to be all right now. "It's fine, I promise. This is Katrina. I've explained everything to her."

I turn the phone around to where the foster mom is waiting anxiously, her hands clasped to her chest. "I'm so sorry!" she says immediately. "I had no idea! Your boyfriend showed me all the photos. Of course you can take Sunny back home. You obviously love her a lot."

"I do," Xander says with a sniffle. "Thank you so much. You're an angel."

I can see that Katrina is still feeling guilty, but she really isn't to blame. I turn the phone back around so I can see my boy. Brig is back, and she's hugging her brother around the neck, staring into the camera. "You found her?" she asks.

I nod, holding Sunny up again. She licks my chin. "Absolutely," I tell them. "I'm on my way to you right now, okay? This will all be over soon. Sunny can't wait to see you."

Xander takes a shaking breath, then nods. "Thank you so much," he whispers.

"Of course, sweetheart," I say. I want to tell him I'd do anything for him. I'd go to the ends of the earth and back again. The least I can do is rescue his beloved fur baby. I can tell him all that later, though, when we're all reunited.

I close the call and sigh, giving Katrina a small smile. "Are you happy for me to take her now?"

Katrina folds her arms and looks disgruntled. "I'm just horrified this happened at all," she says. "I'm going to talk with the company and see if there's anything we can do in the future to safeguard against it."

I shrug. "There are terrible people out there. But I assume you would have taken her to see a vet and scanned her microchip?" She nods, and I give her a bigger smile. "There you go. Xander would have been able to give her number to the police, and I'm sure he would have found her eventually. But at least this way I can get Sunny back to him tonight."

Katrina places her hand over her heart. "He's very lucky to have a boyfriend like you," she says sweetly. "You must love him very much."

I huff out a laugh and look down at Sunny, who looks back up at me, too. "I really do love him that much," I say.

And it's probably way overdue that I told him that.

CHAPTER 21

Xander

I'M SITTING ON THE FLOOR OF MY SOULLESS BEDROOM WITH Brig, the door firmly locked. We heard Felicia go whining to my dad about how unfair I was being over all this, and he basically told her to stop creating drama.

He's charming until it inconveniences him, you see.

Felicia's wrath only increased from that point, so I grabbed Brig, and we ran up to my room to hide until we heard back from Ruben.

I'm still shaking from the relief of seeing him with Sunny. But I know I won't truly believe she's okay until I have her back in my arms. I keep ricocheting between feeling hopeful that everything's going to be all right to imagining all the terrible scenarios that could have been. Not just that I'd never see her again, but that she'd get lost in the back of a shelter once more, or end up in a mean home, or…or…

Brig has been good at keeping me calm. She's crazy mature for her age, but I hate that. As someone who never got to enjoy being a kid myself, I want her to be free to have fun and play. I think she's made of sterner stuff than me, however. Right now, I can't help but lean on her. I just hope one day I'll be able to return the favor.

"That's a car," she says suddenly, perking up just like Sunny does. That almost makes me lose it again, but then I realize that means it's probably Ruben, and I rally immediately. He texted before he left to say that he had his key and he'd let himself in. I almost dare Felicia to try and stop him. But I don't hear any commotion until there's a knock on my bedroom door.

"Xander?" Ruben says.

I lunge to my feet, dashing to the door and hastily scrabbling to unlock it. The second I see Sunny, I drop to the carpet so she can rush into my arms. I burst into tears again, and I don't care in the slightest. There's no room for embarrassment. Only relief.

"It's okay! It's okay!" I say over and over again as she anxiously jumps all over my thighs and licks my face. "You're home. Daddy's here. Uncle Ruben rescued you."

After a minute or so, I realize that Ruben is stranded out in the hallway, so I shuffle backward. He steps into my room, closes the door, then sinks to his knees so he can embrace both me and Sunny.

"Everything's going to be all right, sweetheart," he promises me as he rubs my back. "I've got you. I'm here."

"Thank you," I sob, rubbing my messy face with the back of my hand. "Thank you so much."

He kisses the top of my head. "You don't have to thank me, baby. I'd do anything for you."

We stay like that until I manage to calm down. Sunny was trembling against me, but she's also better now. Honestly, what a completely unnecessary ordeal. I knew Felicia was petty, but I'd never have thought she'd sink this low.

"I'm never leaving Sunny here alone again," I say in a sudden flash of fierce defiance.

"You won't have to," Ruben says as if that's obvious. He pulls back and cups the side of my face, looking into my eyes. "You're moving in with me."

My jaw drops open, and I hear Brig gasp. I'd forgotten she was there, to be honest. I look over to see her sitting on my bed, her legs swinging off the side. She's got her phone clutched to her chest as she beams at us.

"Boyfriend goals," she says in a dreamy voice.

I look back at Ruben, though, my eyebrows raised. "You really want me to move in?" I say quietly. "We haven't been dating long. I don't want to be a burden. Don't feel like you have to."

I can hear the panic rising in my voice, but Ruben just laughs kindly and shakes his head. "Xander, you already have your own room." He doesn't elaborate, obviously, because Brig is with us. But we both know what he means. "I've hated knowing you're living here with people who don't respect you. I wanted to ask you to move in pretty much as soon as we started dating, but I didn't want to pressure you. That's changed now." His face darkens. "You and Sunny aren't safe here." He mellows again and looks at me with such tenderness. "It would be my honor, my pleasure, to have you come live with me."

I bite my lip as a couple more tears tumble down my face. "In that case," I whisper, "I'd love to. But what about you, Brig?"

I turn to look at my sister, and she lifts her eyebrows. "What about me?"

"Will you be all right here alone?"

She blows a raspberry and laughs. "I love you, Xan, but I was just fine before you came back at Christmas. Besides, why do you think I was filming everything this evening?"

"You were?" Ruben asks.

She nods and holds up her phone. "I filmed Mom being a

B-word earlier and Xander getting upset, then calling you. I filmed her yelling and all that. Then I filmed when you came in just now and Sunny was reunited with Xander."

"I thought you were recording in case we needed to go to the police?" I say.

She shrugs. "That too. But now I have all the footage I need for a truly viral TikTok. She'd *hate* it if everyone saw what she was really like."

"That's an understatement," I mumble.

But Brig just grins. "That's why I'm not going to post it unless I have to. I'll cut it together, then save it in a few secret places. But I'll make it clear to Mom that if she ever pulls any kind of BS like that again, I can upload it with just a few clicks." She preens at her own diabolical plan. "I have insurance. I'll be fine now."

I can't help but chuckle in disbelief. "No more surprise beauty pageants for you, then."

"Nope," she agrees, popping the *p*. "So don't you be worrying about me. I'm great. And you've got an awesome boyfriend to be moving in with."

I look back at him and smile shyly. "A *roar*-some boyfriend," I say. I want to call him Daddy, but that can wait. Right now, I'm just so lucky to have him in my life, and two siblings who love him almost as much as I do. I can survive using different words around other people.

Ruben and I both know in our hearts that he's my Daddy and I'm his good baby boy.

He kisses me on the cheek, keeping it PG-rated for the sake of my sister, but I still feel the warmth and affection clear as day.

"Right," he says, brushing his thumb under my eyes to wipe away any lingering tears. "Let's get you packed up, hmm?"

I look down at Sunny and suddenly realize something. "Oh. Did she have any of her things with her?"

Ruben laughs softly. "It's all in the car already, sweetheart. There wasn't any point bringing it in because I knew you'd both be coming home with me along with all your stuff."

I grin at his confidence that I'd say yes to moving in. "Fair enough," I say with a weak chuckle.

Brig jumps off the bed and claps her hands. "Okay, let's pack!" she announces, looking around. "Where are your suitcases?"

"Eager to be rid of me?" I tease. "They're under the bed."

"Yes," she says as she drops down and starts pulling the big one out first. "I am eager to get rid of you because you're making kissy-kissy faces at each other, and it's gross."

Ruben and I both laugh at that, unable to deny it. I do feel so much love for him, not just in this moment, but always. I think my instincts are right. This has got to be love. I can see why people write so many songs about it. It's all consuming and joyous. I feel like I could power the whole of Paddle Creek with all this electricity that's running through me.

I know I need to get up and start getting my clothes from the closet and the chest of drawers. I don't want to stay in this horrible place a minute longer than I have to. But I cling on to Ruben just a little longer. He's my home, my anchor, my port in a storm. In all those hours I spent daydreaming about him as a teenager, I never imagined he'd turn out to be quite this amazing. I feel so incredibly lucky that our paths crossed again and the universe gave us a chance to see what we could accomplish together.

It's not like getting kicked out of my old apartment and having to switch schools was a breeze. And the last few months living under this roof have been a nightmare on for mental health. But nothing good in life is easy, and it feels like I had to get through those trials to make it out the other side and find so much happiness.

And not just with Ruben. I've been so much happier at Paddle Creek College, making friends, and soon I'll finally reach the end of my degree. I grew up in this town, so it's kind of strange that it's only just starting to feel like home in my mid-twenties, but I guess it's better late than never.

Moving in with Ruben is just the beginning. My life is truly starting as of now.

And I can't wait.

CHAPTER 22

Ruben

MY HEART ACHES FOR EVERYTHING MY BOY HAS BEEN THROUGH tonight, but my pain will have to wait till later. Right now, my mission is very clear, and that's to make sure that all of Xander's needs are taken care of down to the tiniest one.

It doesn't take long to pack away all his stuff from his room. I get the impression that he doesn't have many worldly possessions because he's never felt like he belonged anywhere. That's all changing tonight. I want my home to be his home. I want to see his presence in every single room. I want our lives to be so intertwined that he never once doubts again that he has a place in this world.

It's by my side. Flourishing.

He crashes hard on the car ride over to my place. I think the emotional goodbye with his sister was the last straw on his already frayed nerves. He doesn't say a word the whole drive, just cuddles Sunny to his chest. I don't trouble him with any conversation, but I do keep my hand on his knee as much as I can, gently rubbing my thumb against his leg.

Once I park, I tell him to sit tight. I get out so I can open his door and release his seat belt. Then I gently help him out of the car. I'd carry him, but he's clearly dead set on keeping a hold of Sunny, so I wrap my arm around his back instead and guide him toward the door.

The dinner I was cooking is long ruined, but that doesn't matter. It's getting late anyway, so I'll just fix him up something simple. First things first, though, I lay Xander down on the couch and make sure he and Sunny are comfortably curled up together.

Then I rush back out to the truck and start unloading his stuff. It takes a few trips back and forth, but eventually, I get all of his belongings into the hallway. It can stay there for now. Between what he already has here for staying over and his backpack from school with his charger and the like, we have everything he needs readily available for tonight. Tomorrow, we can properly unpack and make sure he feels like he's truly home.

I go back into the living room and crouch down in front of the sofa. He sleepily blinks his eyes open for me. "Dada?" he mumbles.

My heart melts. "Hey, Lally," I say as I brush back his hair. "Are you hungry?" He shrugs, but that's okay. I'm here to make all the decisions. "How about dino nuggets and sweet potato fries? You can take a bath while they cook in the oven."

He nibbles on his lip before nodding. "That sounds nice, Dada."

"Good boy," I tell him. "Let's get you upstairs, okay?"

I help him to stand, and hold his hand as we head up to the bathroom. I have a huge tub that I rarely utilize, as the shower in my en suite is more practical, but I'm hoping now that Xander's going to be here all the time, that it'll get a lot more use.

I get the water going nice and hot and add a shit ton of bubble bath. The air is soon steamy and smelling sweet.

Sunny settles herself in the corner by the radiator, apparently happy so long as she's near Xander. The poor baby is rattled, but she actually has no idea what a close call she had today. I'm glad. She—like Xander—should never know that kind of a fright ever again.

As I carefully undress Xander, he's like a zombie, just swaying on the spot and staring at the wall. We've made so much progress since he moved back into town, so I'm hoping this trauma tonight will just be a blip for him and his confidence. I want to see my baby happy and thriving again soon. But for tonight, I understand that he's in shock and is going to need extra special care.

"Okay, Lally," I say once his clothes are all off. I take his hand and turn him around to face the tub. I dip my fingers in the water to check the temperature, and am pleased that it's just right. "In you get, sweetheart. You just relax now."

He steps in and groans, quickly sinking below the suds. His face lights up when I get a box of toys out of the cupboard. There are a few dinosaurs in there, but also sea life like crabs and turtles, as well as a couple of mermaids. I've been saving them as a surprise for a special occasion. This wasn't what I had in mind, but I'm very glad for the happy distraction I can offer him now. He eagerly takes the collection like it's a chest of plastic treasure.

"Thank you, Dada!" he squeaks, and warmth fills my chest. He's already letting go of all the horrible things his stepmother put him through this evening.

For a while, I just sit and watch him play. He's beautifully un-self-conscious as he chatters away to himself, making up a story about the girl mermaid saving pink fish from the jaws of a T-rex with her friends, the starfish and the pterodactyl. Occasionally, he'll hold one of his toys up and say, "Dada, look!" But for the most part, he's content in his own little world.

It's only because I'm aware of the time that I eventually get up, kiss him on the head, and go down to put his dinner in the oven. I quickly tidy up the mess from the meal I was making before, which occupies me until I need to flip over the nuggies and fries to continue cooking. After that, I head back upstairs.

"Okay, sweet boy," I say as I enter the bathroom. "Time to get you out before you turn into a prune."

"Aww, five more minutes, Dada?"

He pouts up at me, and I have to laugh. "The water's getting cold, baby boy. Come on. Let's get you dry and in your jammies. Then you can have your dino nuggets, and Dada can read you a story."

His face lights up, and my heart melts for the thousandth time. This boy is too sweet, too pure, too perfect. I feel like I've been waiting my whole life to find him.

"Okay, Dada," he says cheerfully before scooping up all his toys and putting them back in the basket. He really is so good.

I make sure every inch of him is dry with a big fluffy towel. I love intimate exchanges like this. I know he's naked, but there's nothing sexual in this moment. It's all just tenderness as I care for his every need.

He's got a few pairs of pajamas now, but tonight I dress him in his original dinosaur pair that I first gifted him with. I get him snuggled in the playroom bed, then jog downstairs to plate up his food. I'll fix myself something later, but right now, I just care about him.

After quickly microwaving some veggies to add to the chicken and potato, I season it the way I know he likes and add a small lake of ketchup. Then I grab his special cutlery and dinner tray and take it all upstairs.

He's still in bed where I left him with Sunny by his feet. He's cuddling his stuffy, Lulu, and staring into space, but he's animated again as soon as I come through the door. I love that when he's in little mode, he never wants to look at his phone. I'm certain the break from doom-scrolling social media does him a lot of good.

"Yum!" he cries as I set him up with his tray and food. "Can I have the mouse story, Dada?"

I smile and pull up the stool I added to the room a while ago. We've read this picture book about the intrepid mouse several times, but I love that he doesn't get bored with it.

The way he wolfs down his dinner as I read assures me that I was correct. I knew he was starving. It's just his brain wasn't getting the right signals after having such a fright. By the time I finish the story, his plate is practically licked clean, and his eyelids are starting to droop.

"Okay, Lally," I say as I slide the book back onto its shelf. "Let's get your teeth brushed, and then you can snuggle down."

"I'm not tired," he says, immediately following his words with an enormous yawn.

I chuckle. "Sure, baby," I say humorously. "Come on. Do it for Dada. You're a good boy, aren't you?"

He nods eagerly and throws the covers back to jump out of bed. "I am, Dada. I'll brush my teeth super hard."

"Not too hard," I call after him as he races down the hall back into the bathroom. By the time I slowly catch up to him, he's already got toothpaste on the electric brush that he switches on and shoves into his mouth. I sit next to him on the closed toilet lid and rub his lower back as he gives his mouth a thorough clean. "Good boy," I murmur.

It hits me in that moment that this is our life now. He lives here. This is his home, and I get to take care of him from the moment he wakes up to the moment he falls asleep. And I just know that this isn't a phase. He's not going to grow out of needing a Daddy like my ex did. He's becoming a more truer version of himself the more he embraces his little side. He's my ray of sunshine, my reason for being.

I was right when I told Joe about me and Xander being together. I'm his king, and I'm going to treat him like the prince he is.

Maybe forever.

I want to tell him that I love him so badly, but I don't want to do it when he's been so shaken and is happily in little head space recovering. But soon.

Soon this perfect boy is going to know that he's my whole world and I'll go to the ends of the earth for him.

Always.

CHAPTER 23

Xander

I'M DISORIENTED WHEN I WAKE. I WAS SLEEPING SO HEAVILY that it takes me several seconds to work out where I am and what's happening. I've napped in my playroom bed before, but never stayed the whole night.

Then I suddenly remember why.

Sunny is curled up asleep by my side, and I quickly wrap my arms around her. I don't want to disturb her, but I also need to reassure myself that she's okay.

I can't believe that Felicia did that to me. I always knew she was bigoted and mean, but giving Sunny away like that was downright sociopathic. I used to think she was mostly harmless. Now I see her for what she really is.

Evil.

But here's the thing about my life these days. There might be bad, but there is also an abundance of so much good, and for that, I am eternally grateful.

On the nightstand beside the bed is a glass of water as well as a folded-up note addressed to me—Xander rather than Lally. I grab the drink first, eager to wet my throat, but also wanting to build up the anticipation of reading whatever

Ruben's written to me. Butterflies dance in my tummy as I unfold the piece of paper.

That's why I'm really convinced this is love. He's my boyfriend, my partner, my Daddy. A sure thing. I shouldn't have to be excited or nervous about getting a message from him.

And yet I'm still both.

It's like any connection with him is a gift that still thrills me, and I'm determined not to take any of it for granted, no matter how long this relationship lasts.

I hope that's a very long time indeed.

Sweet baby boy, the hand-written note begins. *You looked so peaceful that I didn't want to disturb you. But when you wake up, feel free to come and join me if you want. If you're not next door when I wake up, I'll head downstairs and make us pancakes. I won't leave the house before I see you, but please take all the time you need if you'd prefer to be alone for a while. Big hugs, Daddy xxx*

I bite my lip and clutch the note to my chest. He understands me so well it's almost scary. He knew that I'd be anxious about where he was and what I should do, so he laid out all the options for me.

Ironically, he's made me feel so safe and secure, there's only one thing I want. And that's to see him as soon as possible.

First things first, though, I quietly jog downstairs with Sunny at my heel to let her outside to relieve herself and then come back inside to sort her food out. We can take her on a long walk later, but right now, her daddy and my Daddy need some alone time.

"Be a good girl," I whisper to her as I give her a chew stick. Luckily, that seems to do the trick, and I leave her in the kitchen, happily munching away.

I swiftly dash back up to my playroom, pulling off my

pajamas and slipping them under my pillows. Then I grab a pair of briefs to keep a little bit of anticipation going before creeping into Daddy's bedroom.

I guess it's our bedroom now. How amazing is that?

The curtains are still shut, and it's dark inside. I close the door so the daylight from the hallway doesn't disturb Ruben. Then I carefully make my way over to the bed and gingerly pull back the covers just enough so I can slide myself under them. I snuggle up next to my Daddy's hot, solid body, draping my arm around his tummy and hooking my leg over his. He's sleeping on his back, but he must sense me, as he rolls onto his side, flinging his arm over, and hauling me even closer to him.

I grin in the gloom, loving that even when he's unconscious, he still looks after me. I am one lucky boy.

For a while, I doze in his arms, just loving the sound of his breathing and the heat of his skin against mine. But then he starts to stir, running his hand up and down my side and grinding his morning wood against my hip. I try not to giggle in my excitement. We've had all kinds of sex now, but every time it's just as exhilarating. I'm insatiable for him. The fact that he seems to feel the same about me is as unbelievable to me as it is amazing.

I never thought I'd feel desired like this.

Ruben hums and sleepily starts kissing my neck. "Hey, baby boy," he mumbles.

"Morning, Daddy," I say sweetly, wriggling against him. I don't know if it's the residual adrenaline from yesterday or me getting hyper every time I remember that Ruben has asked me to move in permanently, but damn, I'm horny as fuck right now.

I feel him smiling against my throat before he kisses along my jaw and then finds my mouth. "Gorgeous boy," he says, taking a second to pull his T-shirt off so we're both in just our briefs. I love feeling his furry chest against mine. His lips attack mine again with more ferocity, pushing his tongue inside my mouth as his hands drag across my back. "Mine," he growls. "My baby boy. All mine. Such a good boy."

Those words melt over me like butter. I squirm under him as he rolls on top of me. We both fumble together as we're kissing and shoving down our underwear until there's nothing left between us.

"I want you inside me," I say desperately. I need to be as connected as two human beings can be.

"I've got you, baby boy," he says. "Daddy's here. Let me take care of everything."

He gets out the lube that we've been making good use of over the past few weeks. But before he can open the tube, I catch his wrist and still his hand, looking him in the eyes. I've just realized there is a way we can be deeper connected. I know I've probably been waiting for him to make the first move, but sometimes I think it's okay for me to be bold and forward too if it means we can become closer as a couple.

"I love you, Daddy," I say in little more than a whisper. But they're probably the loudest, most powerful words I've ever spoken.

His jaw drops, and he lets out a little "oh" noise. He places the bottle down on the mattress before cupping his hand to the side of my face. "I love you too, baby boy. I wanted to tell you for so long, but I didn't want to overwhelm you."

I snort, a moment of levity in an otherwise serious confession. "A part of me has loved you for, like, a decade, so I'm not sure which of us is worse for bottling it up."

He grins and kisses my mouth tenderly. "It's okay. The past doesn't matter now. Only our future. Together."

Warmth blossoms in my chest at the promise, but I can't help but be a little cheeky as well.

"And the present?" I ask as I grind my cock against his,

making him groan. "I'm still quite interested in what's happening right now."

He chuckles darkly before capturing my lower lip between his teeth and dragging it through. "Oh, don't you worry about a thing, sweetheart. Daddy's got you. Let him take care of everything. You lie on your tummy now and just relax."

It's hard to relax when my dick is leaking and throbbing, but I do as I'm told anyway, flipping over fast, as I'm eager to please my Daddy. Sure enough he runs his hand over my ass cheek and kisses my shoulder blade. "Good boy."

I shiver as he leaves a trail of kisses down my spine. I bury my face against the crook of my arm, my eyes closed so I can focus more on every touch he gives me. I can smell our arousal in the air, and listen as his wet lips connect with my skin.

Then he takes both my cheeks and pulls them apart, gently blowing against my hole.

I squeak and moan, digging my fingers into the mattress. We had penetrative sex a few times, but this is the first time he's ever teased me down there.

And—*oh*—does he tease. He begins by kissing my hole and flicking his tongue out to give my tight entrance little delicious licks. The noises I'm making against my elbow are obscene. He's not really trying to stretch me out. I can tell he's just doing it to pleasure me, and wow is it working. I grind against the mattress, desperate for friction but not getting enough. The torture is kind of glorious, though.

It's as if he's telling me with his body that there's no rush for us anymore. This is my home now and the start of our life together. We can take all the time in the world to make love whenever we want.

Eventually, when I'm a puddle of goo on the bed, he pulls back and reaches for the lube. He must have relaxed me more than I thought, as he's quite easily able to push a couple of fingers inside me, getting me ready for his cock.

We usually have sex with me on my back and him on top, but today he keeps me on my front, lifting my hips so I'm on my knees as he forces his way past my tight ring of muscle. I know from previous experience this can feel absolutely amazing, and as he goes deeper and deeper inside me, I already appreciate it's going to be spectacular. The angle is just perfect as he begins to slide in and out, hitting my sweet spot and making me wail. It's primal and desperate and beautiful.

"Good boy," he grunts as he fucks me harder and faster. "Good boy, so perfect for Daddy. So good. That's it. Take it just like that."

I'm basically sobbing as my orgasm builds. I'm sure left-over emotion from the night before is also catching up with me, but I feel like I'm floating on another plane of existence as I begin to unravel. When Ruben reaches around and starts jerking me off, I'm exploding within a matter of seconds.

I scream and gnash my teeth as I spurt all over his hand and the bedsheets. I can feel him pulsing inside me. I love it when we come together.

When we both stop shaking, he wraps his arms around me and rolls us to the side so we can lie together away from the wet spot. He's softening inside me but not making any move to pull out just yet. I cling to him as I gasp for air, feeling content down to my bones.

"I love you, Daddy," I manage to whisper.

He kisses the side of my neck. "I love you, baby boy."

It doesn't feel any less special than when we said it the first time, which is lucky.

Because I intend on saying it every day for a very long time.

CHAPTER 24

Ruben

PROUD DOESN'T EVEN BEGIN TO COVER IT.

I holler and yell, using two fingers to whistle extra loud when I'm not clapping so hard that my hands are stinging. Xander is quite far away on the stage, receiving his graduation diploma, but I want him to know exactly where I am.

That he's not alone.

He shakes the hand of the person who's just handed him the roll of paper, and my heart leaps as he looks out over the sea of people and smiles directly at me.

That's my baby boy.

On my left, Joe and Zoe are creating just as much of a racket. To my right, Brig has climbed up onto her chair and is filming everything with a grin on her face from ear to ear. My heart swells, knowing my sweetheart is so loved.

Of course, his dad and stepmom aren't here. He was ready to make it very clear that they weren't invited, but luckily (or sadly, depending on how you look at it), they rather obviously announced they had plans on this particular day before the subject even came up. I'm absolutely certain they did it on purpose to save everyone face, but it still cuts me that they really have so much disdain for my darling boy.

Well, that's their choice. If they don't want to be in his life, then he's better off without them, quite frankly. He has his family right here, and none of us could be happier that he's managed such an achievement. He's graduated college, and no one can ever take that away from him.

I glance up at the sky, knowing that if his mom were still with us, she'd be just as proud of him as we all are.

As he leaves the stage, we calm our applause down again to a more demure level, and I give Brig a hand to clamber back off her seat once more. Apparently, her life has been a great deal more bearable over the past couple of months. Felicia has been smart for once in her life and taken her daughter's threat about posting the Sunny video very seriously. And it's kind of crazy because all the kid wants is to be left alone to study. Now she can do that without being forced into activities she hates just because Felicia wishes she had a daughter more like herself. In any case, it meant there was no question that Brig could be here today to support her big brother.

We watch patiently as the rest of the students from Xander's class accept their diplomas one by one. I recognize a few names from the stories he's told me, and give those kids extra loud cheers as well. It's kind of silly, I know, but I'm just as proud of how many friends my sweet boy has made as much as I am for him finishing his education. In the six months he's been back in town, he's flourished into an almost unrecognizable version of himself.

I like to think I had quite a large part in helping him do that.

Him moving into my place was the best decision, and to be honest, the only regret I have is that we didn't do it sooner. But I do acknowledge that even though it was traumatic, there was a part of Xander that needed to see proof of just how callous his stepmother is. Otherwise, I think he'd always have held on to the hope that if he could just prove himself and be good enough, one day she would finally love and respect him.

Now, he's let go of that idea because it's never going to happen. Besides, he doesn't need her love or respect. He has more than he needs from the four people sitting right here, showing their loyalty to him on one of the most significant days of his life.

I like that I can include Zoe in that number. She's definitely a keeper. And it's not just me guessing that. Joe and I got super drunk a few weeks ago, and he admitted that he's pretty sure she's the one.

It made it easier for me to confess that I think Xander is the one as well. I'd been a little nervous to admit that, although I guess that's the ultimate proof that I'm going to treat his little brother right. Any fears I had were alleviated when he joked that the only problem with that was he wouldn't know who he should be the best man for.

I'm musing on that thought when I realize the ceremony is over and people are starting to get up from their seats. The four of us shuffle down until we reach the aisle and start making our way out the back. It's a beautiful spring day, so it's not a problem to wait around for Xander to come find us.

It doesn't take him long. Just like every time I see him, my heart skips a beat as his familiar form emerges from the crowd. He looks so handsome in his cap and gown that it takes my breath away. I took about a hundred photos this morning, including ones with Sunny, so we had to brush him down after to make sure we got all her caramel fur off. It's going to be a struggle to pick which ones I want to frame and put on the wall alongside his official portrait, but that's a problem I'm very happy and privileged to have.

"Ruben!" he cries as he throws himself into my arms. I know he'd prefer to call me Daddy, but that's something private between us. It's the word I hear in my mind regardless.

I squeeze him tight and rub his back. "You did awesome, sweetheart."

He scoffs. "All I did was stand on stage for a few seconds," he says with a blush.

I give him a stern look. "After working your ass off for several years," I say pointedly.

"Just take the compliment, bro," Joe says, clapping him on the arm and grinning widely. "Damn, you did good!"

"He definitely did," says another voice. I look up to see a couple of guys approaching us. It takes me a second to recognize them out of uniform. Usually, they're just little blips on the playing field to me.

The first guy sticks his hand out at me. "You must be Ruben," he says, an unmistakable air of dominance about him. Not in a combative way. The young man just radiates authority.

I shake his hand. "And you must be Seth. Xander's told me a lot about you."

"Likewise," he says back, and I appreciate in that moment we're talking Daddy to Daddy. His style might be different than mine, but I can still tell.

Speaking of different styles, the other young man comes across a lot more like a giant puppy dog as he also shakes my hand, crushing it slightly in his enthusiasm. "Hello, sir. I'm Marty," he says as he lets me go. I know what his name is, but I appreciate his good manners. "It's so great you were able to be here for Xander today. Our boyfriend, Gabe, is here as well! We should go find him soon."

"We will, big man," Seth assures him with deep fondness as he bumps his shoulder against the taller guy's arm. He then turns to Xander and also shakes his hand. "I'm real glad that Professor Knight put us together for that project. You stay in touch now, you hear?"

"Definitely," Xander says breathlessly.

I know my baby boy still doesn't fully believe that the 'cool kids' like him and honestly consider him a friend. But he doesn't see that when you're a genuine and kind person, it attracts people with no time for bullshit. The Daddy in me is thrilled that he's got buddies now who value him, and I'm sure they'd have his back if he ever needed it.

"You coming to Creams later?" Marty asks. Then he glances at me. "You'd be totally welcome too of course," he adds earnestly. "It'll be epic. I think pretty much every queer graduating student's gonna be there."

I have to admit that the town's gay bar isn't usually my scene. I'm not a dancer, and the music's typically too loud for talking. But when Xander glances hopefully at me, I don't hesitate. "Hell yeah," I assure him. "That sounds like fun."

"And you guys?" Xander asks Joe and Zoe.

"Sure," Zoe says with a nod. "I love a bit of Creams. We can celebrate in style."

"Can *I* come?" Brig demands, looking up at all the adults.

That gets a laugh for us, but Joe's the first to give her a sympathetic look. I remember it wasn't that many years ago that Xander was the one begging to hang out with us.

Look at him now.

"I'm afraid it's a place just for grown-ups," Joe tells his little sister. "But we're all going to go together to dinner now, so you're not missing out on anything important, I promise!"

She narrows her eyes at him in consideration. "Hmm, okay," she says. "But I'm getting a chocolate milkshake."

"A large one, I promise!" Joe tells her.

We say good-bye to Seth and Marty. Apparently, both their families are here along with Gabe, and all of them are going to a fancy place for their dinner. I told Xander we could go anywhere he wanted to celebrate, no matter the cost.

He chose Dino-Mite.

If Joe or Zoe thought it was weird that he wanted to go to his workplace, they haven't mentioned it to me. In fact, they got really into the spirit of it all, saying it would be fun. Brig has been brushing up on her paleontology for the last couple of days.

But I know my boy. He's got a fancy degree now, and he could try for all kinds of jobs, but he confessed to me a little while ago that—at least for now—he's more than happy to keep working at the restaurant. Maybe even take on some more hours and responsibilities. It might be tacky and dated, but he loves it there, surrounded by all his prehistoric friends. So if that's where he wants to mark this important occasion, that's what we'll do.

I'll do anything for him. It's been my absolute honor to see him flourish over these past several months. I know things are only going to keep getting better for him, too. I think that's why this graduation was so pivotal. It's not just proving that he's completed his degree. This moment marks a new chapter for him. He's moving on from his old life, where he was made to feel worthless and like he was taking up too much space. Now he's starting to see his value and just how loved he is by so many people.

First and foremost by me.

Epilogue

TWO AND A HALF YEARS LATER – XANDER

"Whoa, that's a lot of stuff!" Ruben calls from the front porch. He dashes out into the snow with Sunny at his heels, hurrying to help me.

"I got a bit carried away," I groan as I gratefully hand him the bags I've just gotten out of the car. I love that he must have been watching out the window to see me pull into our driveway. Even after all this time, he's still eager and anxious to help me. "No peeking, though!" I threaten as he unburdens me of the Christmas presents that I managed to buy this afternoon. Some of them are for him, after all.

I love this time of year now. It used to be hard for me as—like a lot of holidays—it's a celebration that really focuses on family. For so long, I was made to feel completely unwelcome in that house that was supposed to be my home.

Now I feel treasured all the time, but especially during the holidays. Ruben still lights up whenever he sees me, making me feel like a rock star. He always goes all out when it comes to presents and special treats. This Christmas, I wanted to at least try to spoil him as well, but knowing him,

I'll still be hopelessly outdone. That's okay, though. That's why he's the best Daddy.

I have presents for Brig, Joe, and Zoe as well, and I made sure to put them on top so Ruben wouldn't see anything of his when I got back to the house. It's still a week before Christmas, so I've got enough time to wrap everything. In fact, I realized earlier today that it's the three year anniversary of me moving back to Paddle Creek.

That means it's three years to the day since Ruben came back into my life. I wonder if he's remembered. I grin to myself as I head into the house, pondering if there's a sexy way I can remind him of the fact later this evening.

I'm almost on the porch when I realize that Ruben's already taken the shopping bags inside the house and is waiting for me as he holds the door open with Sunny at his feet. I jog up the steps, not wanting to let too much cold air in, but pause as I reach the front door.

There's a dinosaur footprint on the floor. It looks like glittery black sand has been shaken onto the carpet using a stencil, or at least that would be my guess. There are a couple more that lead toward the stairs, and from what I can see at this angle, there are more going upward as well.

I look at Ruben with a confused frown, but he just grins at me and rocks on his feet. Sunny's being very good and sitting by his feet, but she wags her tail excitedly when I glance their way.

"What's that, baby boy?" Ruben asks in his cute Daddy voice. I wasn't feeling particularly in a little mood, but his tone makes me laugh, a thrill rushing through my body.

"Dinosaur?" I say as I close the door. I kick my shoes off, and he automatically reaches out to take my coat.

"Why don't you see where the dinosaur went?" he suggests. He's brimming with excitement and I have to admit that my curiosity is piqued. It's not unusual for him to be delighted by my or Lally's enthusiasm for something, but it's like he can't contain himself right now.

I bite my lip and carefully start to follow the trail of footprints without disturbing the black sand. There are three fat toes, each with small claws at the tips, which makes me think of a T-rex. It would have to be a baby one to fit in the house, and I can't help but grin as my imagination runs away with me, thinking how fun it would be to have my very own pet dinosaur. I bet Sunny would love that. Of course in my imagination, my new pet dino would never hurt my baby girl.

My anticipation grows as I reach the landing and see that the footprints lead up to my playroom. The door is closed like usual. We never bother locking it aside from the rare occasions we have people over to visit, but I like it closed so we only open it for Lally. That keeps it more special, I think. Today, though, I'm not sure what to expect as I dart across the landing and turn the door handle with Ruben following behind me.

I gasp.

It's dark outside and the main light is turned off, but that just emphasizes that Ruben has strung up fairy lights over the whole room. There are also flower petals strewn over the floor and every other available surface, but they're not roses like I might have assumed. They're a riot of color like you'd find in a tropical rainforest, all orange, purple, blue, and pink. Several candles in glass jars are positioned amid the petals. Sparkly green streamers hang from the ceiling that I gently push aside to get to the bed.

Because sitting on it is a giant T-rex stuffy. I was right—the footprints *did* belong to a baby T-rex! I also notice that in the corners of the small room there are two helium balloons in the shape of pterodactyls. I giggle, feeling both nervous and excited.

"Do you know what today is, baby boy?" Ruben asks

quietly. I turn around to see him standing at the threshold. It reminds me of when he showed me this room for the very first time. That seems so long ago now.

I clutch my hands to my chest. I should have known he'd remember without me having to tell him. "It's the day we met again three years ago."

His expression is so warm and full of love. "That's right, sweetheart. You're such a clever boy." I blush at the praise. Even after all this time together, it still means so much to me.

"I love it, Daddy. Thank you."

He surprises me by shaking his head. "That's not all, baby. Why don't you see what your new friend is holding?"

I turn back to the T-rex and see that he's right. I hadn't spotted it before, but her hands are tied together with a bow, and between them is a little box. I creep through the rest of the streamers, making them rustle around me, and reach out to carefully extract the box.

My heart is thumping in my chest. Crazy thoughts are flying around my head. I want to jump to conclusions, but I'm afraid I'll be wrong. Instead, I turn back around to ask Ruben what's going on.

I find him in front of me, waiting on one knee.

I gasp, one hand flying over my mouth, the other clutching so tightly to the box that the corners are biting into my palm. He reaches out and slides his hands over mine, gently easing the box out of my grip. I'm not breathing. Even Sunny is being totally quiet where she's waiting on the landing. So when Ruben cracks the box open, it seems very loud to my ears.

Nestled inside is a silver-looking ring with an oval amber centerpiece. The band is thick but delicate tendrils swirl around the stone. When I peer closer, I realize that there's a darkened image of a mosquito in the orange gem, just like the one they make the dinosaurs from in the Jurassic Park movies.

I immediately realize that it symbolizes a new beginning. The creation of something...*spectacular.*

That's all I see before tears fill my eyes and blur out my vision. I feel my Daddy take my hand again, rubbing his thumb against the back, and I laugh as I hastily use my other hand to rub the tears away so I can see him again.

"Oh, Daddy," I mumble, feeling so overwhelmed.

"My sweet boy," he says, looking up at me like I hung the moon. "I love you so very much. I want to spend the rest of my life being your Daddy. Will you marry me?"

The floodgates open, and I can't help but sob as I drop to my knees and throw my arms around him. He hugs me crushingly tight and buries his face against my neck. Sunny finally jumps up from where she's been sitting and races over to us, barking and putting her paws on my shoulder so she can try and lick both our faces. It makes me laugh, and I wouldn't have it any other way.

"Yes!" I manage to croak out to Ruben. "Yes, yes, *yes!*"

I spent so much of my life feeling alone and like I was never meant to be loved. That I was *unlovable*, in fact. And then I met Ruben, and he made me feel like I was the most precious person on the entire planet. I can't imagine the rest of my life without him.

And now I don't have to.

———

Thank you so much for reading Xander and Ruben's story!

The hunt for love is on.

Make sure you don't miss the next Paddle Creek College book featuring fierce Daddy Rick, his wolf pack, Treyvon and Brady, and their brand new pretty little lamb, Harper. Four Play is coming summer 2023.

Pre-order your copy now!

If you want more small towns or Daddies, make sure you keep reading for other books by HJ Welch/Helen Juliet.

———

If you'd like to be the first to know what's happening next in Paddle Creek, make sure to join my Facebook group, **Helen's Jewels**. We also have a lot of fun with games and giveaways, as well as ARC opportunities.

———

Thank you to my team!

Cover Design: Cate Ashwood

Editing: Meg Cooper

Proof Reading: Tanja Ongkiehong

Formatting (and general awesomeness): Ed Davies

Love and support: Hubby and our cats

Also Available

PADDLE CREEK #1: HEAVEN SENT BY HJ WELCH

Two rival jocks. One adorable nerd. A bet that changes everything.

SETH

Being captain of the Paddle Creek Panthers is my life. I wouldn't care that my grades have slipped, except it could not only cost me my shot at the pros, but now the rich kid in town has wagered that if I don't graduate, I'll owe him *big* time. Can this gorgeous little freshman geek Gabe really save my degree and my reputation? All I know is that as soon as I laid eyes on him, I needed him. And I *don't* want to share.

MARTY

I've spent almost four years trying to get my captain Seth to notice me. He's hot as hell and knows how to boss a guy around, even one as big as me. To him, though, I'm just the team clown. But when he drags me into this graduation bet, it's no laughing matter. So why shouldn't this little cherub Gabe tutor me as well? In fact, I don't see why we can't share him in all *kinds* of ways. Seth is clearly a natural Daddy, Gabe thrives being doted on, and I'm happy to Daddy *and* be Daddied. Win-win, right?

GABE

Somehow, I've found myself standing up to the guy whose family pretty much owns Paddle Creek and put my neck on the line for two of the college's star players. Now we're spending every day together as I try and save their grades, and I don't know if I'm crazy but it's like they both *want* me. I've never had a boyfriend. I'm not even out to my overbearing parents. How could I choose between them…or do I actually have to when they *both* want to be my Daddies? After my life comes crashing down, it's their turn to come to my rescue. Maybe what me and these god-like men have isn't just a fling after all?

*Heaven Sent is a steamy, standalone MMM romance. It's the first book in the **Paddle Creek College** series, where it's always the quiet ones who get up to the best kind of trouble. This book features a geek tutoring two hot jocks, two hot jocks tutoring a geek in a completely different way, a trash panda with a heart of gold, a human ice cream sundae, a revenge curse, and a guaranteed HEA with absolutely no cliffhanger.*

Click here to get the Heaven Sent eBook

PADDLE CREEK #2: YES, SIR BY HJ WELCH

Two men. Two secrets. Can true love set them free?

BENEDICT

Just one more year, then I can go back to my beloved Oxford University and leave this tiny town behind me. Teaching is my passion, but I have other desires that I know would get me fired if anyone found out. The only trouble is, my new TA is pushing all my buttons and I'm not sure he even realizes what calling me Sir does to me. That's nothing, however, compared to when he starts calling me Daddy.

JACKSON

Have I got hots for teacher? Oh, yes. Messing around is off the table, though, so in a way it's safe to flirt with him and see him lose that stiff upper lip. It's not like he'd be interested in me anyway if he ever discovered what I love wearing under my clothes. Tough guys like me shouldn't like satin and lace. They shouldn't want to feel pretty. But Sir makes me feel gorgeous, and I want to be *such* a good boy for him.

*Yes, Sir is a steamy, standalone MM romance. It's the second book in the **Paddle Creek College** series, where it's always the quiet ones who get up to the best kind of trouble. This book features two people learning they don't have to be ashamed of who they are, a sassy brat who really wants to behave, a master in the bedroom who's a caring Daddy at heart, role playing so good it could win an Oscar, and a guaranteed HEA with absolutely no cliffhanger.*

Click here to get the Yes, Sir eBook

Also Available

BEARS-4-U (MULTI-AUTHOR SHARED UNIVERSE): KEEP ME BY HJ WELCH

Snowed in for a second chance at love...

BECKETT

It's been over two years since I lost my darling husband, and my best friend is taking matters into her own hands. She's signed me up to a dating app for bears and those that love them, even encouraging me to attend a weekend mixer. I go to humor her, not expecting to rescue the most adorable boy...twice. But I'm not ready to open up my heart again, am I?

LAURIE

My last Daddy was bad news. It's taken a lot of courage for me to reach out on Bears-4-U and go to this mixer, only to find that the new Daddy I've been talking to is just as awful. That's when Beckett swoops into my life like a hero in a story book. I know he's not looking for love, but I want to mend his broken heart so badly. When a scary snowstorm blows in and strands us, I trust he'll keep me safe and warm. I want to be in his life, in his bed, in his heart…forever.

Bears-4-U is a MM Daddy romance multi-author series, featuring a host of delicious Daddy pairings. The Bears-4-U dating app is all about putting Bears and Teddy Bears together for their honey-sweet HEAs. Psst, no real bears involved. Each book can be read as a standalone, but why not snuggle up with all the bears?

Click here to get the Keep Me eBook

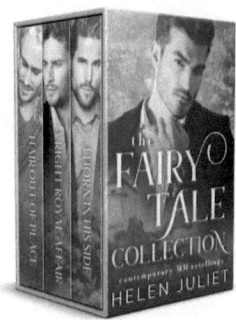

Golden

When Goldie's ex-boyfriend leaves him in serious debt with the adult entertainment company he works for, Goldie gets the chance to work off the money...in front of the camera. The idea excites him, but then his favourite throuple—Daddy, Papa, and Baby —*demand* he comes to play with them. No matter how scared he is, he can't miss this opportunity, not even when his past comes back to haunt him.

———

Wild Ride

When Red is chased into the woods, he seeks sanctuary at his estranged grandma's house. He doesn't expect to be rescued by his older brother's best friend, the man he was always madly in love with. Could Hunter be the Daddy of Red's wildest dreams? Especially when he unlocks a secret passion of Red's for beautiful lingerie. There's still a threat lurking in the woods, though, and Hunter realises he'll do anything to protect his beautiful boy.

———

Three

When three shy best friends sign up to a dating app to finally get some by the end of the year, they don't expect to all fall for the same gorgeous, slightly scary-looking Daddy. The only solution? Let him choose who he wants to bed. Except he doesn't. Daddy Wolf wants to spoil each little piggy, one after another. But when danger comes calling, will their love for each other be enough to save them all?
Includes Halloween bonus scene!

———

Nine Lives

When Charlie suddenly finds himself homeless and penniless, he decides to sell the only thing left he owns. Himself. For the very first time. Lucky for him he stumbles across Miller, the own of a London kink club, who saves him from those who would take advantage of him. As Miller discovers his inner Daddy, he also unlocks Charlie's kitten alter-ego. But with both their families meddling, will new love be enough to keep them together?

Click here to get the Daddy's Fairy Tales eBook bundle

Also Available

PINE COVE BOX SET BY HJ WELCH

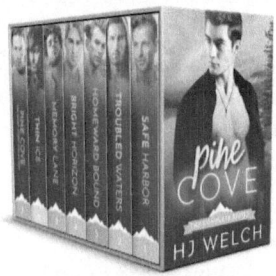

Welcome to Pine Cove, where true love lives happily ever after! **This 2000 page box set contains all six novels as well as all five companion short stories.**

Click here to get the Pine Cove eBook bundle

Click here to get the Pine Cove audio bundle

————

Safe Harbor

Robin Coal needs a fake boyfriend for his high school reunion. He asks his housemate: a gorgeous, totally straight ex-Marine. What could go wrong? There's only one bed, and Dair might not be so straight after all... When Robin's past threatens their future, only Dair can save him.

————

Sweet Spot

It's Halloween and Robin has prepared a sexy little surprise for his boyfriend Dair when he gets home from work. Hold on to your horses, Marine!

———

Troubled Waters

Bodyguard Scout Duffy doesn't know what's worse: the fact that his scorching one-night-stand, Emery Klein, is his bratty new client, or the fact that he doesn't even remember Scout. But Emery's life is in danger thanks to his out and proud charity work, and once he finally recognizes Scout, their chemistry in undeniable.

———

Homeward Bound

Swift Coal just found out he's a father, and his daughter (and her cranky cat) are coming to stay. His best friend's younger brother, Micha Perkins, has nowhere to go and a wrongfully tattered reputation. He's relieved when Swift asks him to be a live-in babysitter. He just has to hide his lifelong crush. Easy, because Swift is straight—right?

———

Bright Horizon

With sixteen years between them, baker Ben Turner and lawyer Elias Solomon have no idea their crush is mutual. But when Ben inherits his long-lost family's estate and becomes an overnight millionaire, Elias swears to protect the innocent younger man from the vultures circling him. To unravel the mystery of the inheritance, they must go to England to confront Ben's estranged relatives…and their feelings for each other.

———

Crossed Paths

Raj Bhat is done living in the shadows. It's time for him to take charge of his own destiny and tell the man he's fallen for how he really feels.

———

Midnight Sky

It's the night before New Year's Eve. Taylan Demir is all alone, and he's just lost his dog. Except when his handsome customer, Hudson Perkins, comes to his rescue, Taylan doesn't just get his dog back. He's suddenly got a hot date, and maybe someone to kiss when the clock strikes midnight.

———

Memory Lane

Angel Shields saved Jay Coal's life in high school, and Jay has secretly loved his straight best friend ever since. Now Angel's back in town with amnesia after a suspicious work accident and it's Jay's turn to rescue him. He pretends to be Angel's fiancé to see him in the hospital, but with his scrambled-up memory, Angel's not sure it's fictional after all. He just knows he loves Jay more than ever.

———

Thin Ice

Kamran's ex broke his heart, tricked him into aiding a bank robbery, and now he wants him to do one last job. There's only one way to say no: seek the protective custody of the biggest, grumpiest FBI agent ever, Lee Marshall. And pretend to be his boyfriend for a week-long family reunion in their giant mansion. Wait, what?

———

Calm Shores

Gorgeous, sophisticated Dante walks into Oliver's bar and orders…a boyfriend?! Dante needs a man to keep his mother from setting him back up with his awful, cheating ex, and Oliver is up for the challenge.

———

Fresh Snow

Emery Klein is throwing the best Christmas party ever, but his fiancé, Scout Duffy, and all their friends have something more exciting in mind.

———

Each Pine Cove book can be read as a stand alone and has its own happy ever after. But if you read the whole series, you'll see a lot of familiar faces!

Click here to get the Pine Cove eBook bundle

Click here to get the Pine Cove audio bundle

About the Author

HJ Welch is an author of contemporary MM romance series, including the international bestselling Pine Cove series. She lives just outside of London with her husband and two balls of fluff that occasionally pretend to be cats. She began writing at an early age, later honing her craft online in the world of fanfiction on sites like Wattpad. Fifteen years and over half a million words later, she sought out original MM novels to read. By the end of 2016 she had written her first book of her own, and in 2017 she achieved her lifelong dream of becoming a full-time author. When she's not writing she's usually dancing, singing, filming music videos, taking long walks, working on jigsaw puzzles, drinking prosecco, or talking about Eurovision.

She also writes contemporary British MM fairy tale adaptations as Helen Juliet.

You can contact Helen via the following:
    Newsletter: https://www.subscribepage.com/helenjuliet
    Website – www.hjwelch.com
    Facebook Group – Helen's Jewels
    Instagram – @helenjwrites
    Twitter – @helenjwrites
    Book Bub – @HJWelchAuthor
    Facebook Page – @HJWelchAuthor

www.ingramcontent.com/pod-product-compliance
Lightning Source LLC
Chambersburg PA
CBHW051224210726
48290CB00003B/786